ISBN 1-58898-708-6

Seas of Enchantment

James R. Field

greatunpublished.com
Title No. 708
2002

Seas of Enchantment

HISTORICAL NOTE

This story is set in medieval Ireland of the early fourteenth century. However, it is not primarily a work of historical fiction, but of fantasy. I have been more free with historical events than a writer of historical fiction might be.

The invasion of Edward Bruce, is, of course, a real event. He was defeated and killed while marching with two thousand Scots and a number of native Irish to attack the English at Dunkalk in 1318. The battle in my story is modelled after these events, but is not meant to be a reconstruction of these events.

The term "middle nation" has been applied to the Anglo Irish who, having been part of the earlier English invasions of Ireland, beginning with Henry II, were then gradually assimilated. They adapted Irish customs and language and in time their loyalty to England grew strained.

Names, such as MacFinn, MacErin, MacFael, O'Leary, Sharlaugh are entirely fanciful.

I

Sir Robert has come to Galway from Kerry to see the Abbot because the Abbot, so they say, is an authority on the Western Seas. They say that as a young man he had sailed them himself. They say that throughout his long life he has collected stories from sailors and fishermen. They say his library boasts such works as the Navigatio Sancti Brendani Abbatis, the story of the voyage of Saint Brendan, and several charts of the Western Seas. The charts show the seas littered with islands like beans in a pot, islands that bear exotic names from legend and mythology: Saint Brendan's Isles, said to be the islands visited long ago by Saint Brendan; Hy-Brasil, professed to be enchanted; Antillia, Island of the Seven Cities; even an island called the Isle of Satan's Hand. And beyond all of this, the "Terra Repromissionis Sanctorum," the Land Promised to the Saints. They say. They say other things as well: the Abbot is mad, the Abbot is a saint, the Abbot can see into the future, the Abbot has a treasure of driftwood collected from the wrack blown by winter storms, including some with mysterious inscriptions, said to have drifted from lands to the west.

Sir Robert is accompanied by his son, Rory, not yet twenty. The Abbot receives Sir Robert in his office, ordering a brother to bring some ale to quench the traveler's thirst. Rory remains outside by the roundhouse with the horses.

The room is dark and the air within stale and dusty. A heavy curtain blocks out the sun; it seems designed to shut out the world and its despair, yet it is itself a symbol of despair. It is a symbol of the Abbot's own despair: a despair which eats away from within.

"I am Sir Robert FitzWalter, son of William FitzWalter."

Sir Robert seldom uses his title of knighthood among the Gaels. The truth is he is ashamed of it. It reminds him that he has made his peace with the English king not from any sense of loyalty (he has fought on both sides) but merely because he is afraid to lose his land. He justifies his action by saying he wanted only to protect his son Rory's patrimony. But Rory himself has little use for English patrimony. A quiet boy, not given to boasting, Rory has nonetheless expressed himself on this subject with great gusto. "I will claim what is mine as an Irish, through Irish law," he boasted, scoffing at the English in their castles

With all this in mind, Sir Robert waits, watching the Abbot's face for some sign of recognition.

"You knew my father."

Perhaps the old man needs coaxing. He is old. So old seemingly to be ageless. He must have been old when he knew Sir William. So many years ago.

"Aye."

So it is not a lack of recognition. It is but prodigious indifference. The indifference of the sage, of one who has already passed beyond— beyond human ties, beyond love, beyond hate, beyond care. This is good. It is what Sir Robert needs.

A flicker of impatience crosses the Abbot's otherwise expressionless face.

"What brings you here?"

"I have a story to tell. Of something happened years ago. The year Edward Bruce was king in Erin."

The Abbot lets out huff, letting it be known he remembers the year, but has little time for the claims of kings, particularly dreamers and schemers like Edward Bruce.

"Is this by way of a confession, then?"

"Not as such, Father. Though there may be much I need confess, I have done so already, and been reconciled. Father Daniel, the priest in Kerry near my home, heard my confession. He sent me hither to speak to you, because you are an authority on the Western Seas—and other things as well."

"This narrative has to do with the Western Seas, then?"

Sir Robert thinks he detects a faint glimmer of awakening interest.

"Aye. It concerns certain islands said to be located in the Western

Seas just upon the horizon, enchanted islands which can be seen only at certain times. Father Daniel says you yourself have seen them once."

Sir Robert smiles at the Abbot, trying to cajole a response from him, but the Abbot remains stone-faced and silent. Sir Robert waits patiently, not wanting to importune. So much depends upon this man of God and his wisdom.

"Many have seen such islands," the Abbot says at last, with an offhand shrug. "Especially the locals; they tell all sorts of fascinating tales about them. From the cliffs of Innismane I have, as you said, often seen them myself. They hang on the horizon like a bank of clouds. Some say that's what they are—no more. Clouds, and men's imagination. One fellow—a fisherman—claimed he was so close he could almost have cast his net over it, but if he did so much as paddle an arm's length closer it would fly away like a flightish bird. The 'Flyaway Islands,' some call them."

The Abbot folds his hands in front of his ancient, ashen face. In the dingy gloom his moist eyes shine like two stars. His right eyelid droops; a wart hangs on the end of it, under a hairy brow. His face betrays no emotion, no trace of the thoughts passing through his mind.

The Abbot had been a young man once, though it is impossible for his visitor to imagine it. He had lived the life of a hermit, following an old practice of the Gaels no longer countenanced by Rome. Like many ascetics he was really no more than a hedonist of the spirit; he chose the most beautiful of sites, a cave in a cliff overlooking the sea, for his home. From there he spent hours gazing westward. It was, he thought, like gazing into the future. The horizon drew his gaze the way the future draws our being; he could not help searching it, but there was nothing to see. There was only a blank, empty space. Sometimes he saw what almost could have been a bank of clouds but which, as he stared, seemed to materialize before his eyes—an island, a piece of land, a separate reality all its own. Some part of him had ached as he stood and beheld the sight before him, drawn to the vision. He could not say why. He could not be sure what he saw was real; it defied what he knew. What he knew was the empty sea, the empty, forbidding, unpredictable sea, the grave of unlucky fishermen, the maker of widows, the bringer of storms, of the ceaseless winter mist and rain—and of rheumatism. That emptiness had awed him all his life. His soul had longed to fill it, and, as if in answer to his secret wish, the vision had appeared.

He knew, or thought he knew, the vision was false. He had been told so by others who had seen it before him. But seeing it then with his own eyes, he could not believe it was false. Such a vision could not be false.

The books, the charts, the tales of fishermen and merchants, the driftwood—these he had collected over the years since, never letting out of his mind the vision that had once enthralled him. It may be this was just his way of filling an emptiness within his own heart. The vision he had seen in the Western Seas spoke to his hope, to his faith, and to his expectations. If it was not real, what was?

So he asked himself.

On other occasions, disenchanted, he cried aloud—"Why do men long for what is not? Why do we not accept what is real but fill our heads with illusions which only disappoint us?"

He asks himself this again, benignly scrutinizing his visitor, seeing now for the first time the resemblance between Sir Robert and his father, Sir William. Then he continues in a subdued, almost nonchalant tone.

"Some men claim the islands are naught but a reflection in the air, and we see merely the image of the self-same land upon which we stand. Others say they are enchanted."

"Aye," Sir Robert says. "I have heard all of that when I was a boy. Yet I was there. I have walked the beaches and the paths, and I have eaten and drunk with the inhabitants, and—I've loved a maiden there whose name was Una."

Una: Una of the dark hair, with the pearl white teeth, the firm white breasts and clear blue eyes. Princess Una: she of ancient lineage, daughter of a great chief, heiress of the sea itself. In her arms he had thought he had discovered paradise. In her eyes he believed he saw worlds. Her eyes could draw a man's soul right out of his body, and her voice—why she had only to speak the most simple words and she could weave a spell and bind a man with his own compulsion more firmly than he could be bound by ropes or chains.

"If they be nothing but a reflection in the air," Sir Robert says, thinking of all this, "then I have passed through the veil of appearances *itself and emerged on the other side. And if they be enchanted, why then so was I."*

And could he not also add that if that were so, then as surely as her island was enchanted, so was Una an enchantress—embroidering fancies upon the fabric of men's desires and imagination. He knows nothing of such things—enchantresses and enchantments—or knew nothing of them prior to his adventure. It can be the term only describes what his mind fails to grasp; like the island which was her home, there was something elusive about the Princess Una.

Not her beauty, mind! There was nothing elusive about that! It was a magic no man could ignore, be there blood in his veins. Yet many women have beauty. What Una had was something harder to describe, something without which beauty is a hollow shell. And that intangible thing, by whatever name you call it, can only be described as enchanting.

Robert observes the Abbot's ashen face, expressionless behind a mask of shadows. The Abbot's indifference whittles away at his patience, until he finally bursts.

"But if you do not believe me, it makes no difference. Why waste my breath? I'll be on my way and trouble you not."

He has had his fill of being called a liar. His is a story good for public houses, poured into ears made receptive by pints of ale. In the morning men laugh and roll their eyes. He is tired of their scorn.

The Abbot makes a motion with his white, liver-spotted hand. He is gesturing for Sir Robert to remain seated, though the gesture, weak and shaky, looks more as if he were clearing away cobwebs.

"No. I pray thee, don't go."

Sir Robert scrutinizes him, narrowing his eyes. For the first time he thinks he detects interest and emotion. The way the Abbot says "No" betrays fear. With surprise Sir Robert realizes that the Abbot, despite his aloof disinterest, is afraid—afraid Robert may leave without telling his story.

"My son," *the Abbot says, composing himself,* "no man wastes his breath who speaks from his heart and believes in Christ."

"Amen," *Sir Robert whispers back.*

2

They were bound for Donegal—a small retinue of men the Irish called a *ceartharnaigh*, or *kern*, usually consisting of at least twenty men. It was made up of lightly-armed Irish mercenaries, and one Norman foot soldier, a man who had fought in the Holy Land and was now unemployed. They had assembled hastily in response to rumors from afar. The English king was making war and all the men of Erin were mustering, some to one side, some to the other.

Robert, not then a knight, was supporting the claim of Edward Bruce to the throne of Ireland. Although Anglo-Norman by descent, several generations of intermarriage (Robert's own mother was Irish) had made Robert more Irish than English or Norman. The king's men in Dublin held no truck with that. They were inclined to support the claims of the *Sasonaigh*—absentee English (or "Saxon") lords who claimed title to Irish lands through English law, and rejected the *Tail male*, or Irish law. Robert's father had fought a bitter feud with the English authorities in Dublin to keep his own lands.

Besides, Robert owed a debt to his brother-in-law O'Leary, who had vouched for him with the Irish chieftains in a dispute with a powerful neighbor. O'Leary asked him to bring a *kern*. Six was all Robert had managed in Kerry, in addition to his foster brother Neill, for whom this was his first "adventure." Robert hoped to gather more in Donegal.

The way by land through Thomond was fraught with danger. Men loyal to the English king and his Viceroy were on the lookout. Friends urged him to wait until a force large enough to ward off attack could be organized; but Robert was not so easily put off. "By then the fighting will be over," he said. Finding a ship bound for Donegal he paid the pilot, a leather-skinned maritimer named Tom, to take them aboard.

The ship was named *Black Sligo*. "*Black* she is called," the pilot, Tom, said, "Seein' so much tar's been put on her to keep her from leaking. And *Sligo*, seein' she hails from there, as it please you, sir."

Robert left behind a wife, O'Leary's sister, Maire, eight months pregnant.

It was a matter of indifference to Robert where the ship hailed from, so long as it got them to Donegal, he said, and with this practical observation he entrusted his fate to the protection of *Black Sligo's* stout timbers and her pilot's wisdom and experience.

Somewhere out of Galway they encountered a thick and heavy fog—"a vile sickness," Tom, called it, a dark veil like the cataracts of a blind man's eyes. Blind they were too, and adrift, there being not the slightest breeze or puff of wind.

For three days and nights they drifted and even Tom admitted he had no means of knowing where they were. He worried that the current might carry them towards land, and wreck them upon unknown shores, perhaps never to see their homes and family again. He recalled tales he had heard of islands where the inhabitants preyed upon shipwrecks, murdering the survivors so they might be free to plunder the wreck. And an island called "Isle of Satan's Hand" that would appear mysteriously, wrapped in a chilly mist, where previously no island had been seen.

"I say 'appeared,' but in truth, men never saw anything but dark shadows, though they could hear splashing water and lapping waves, as of the sea against a rocky shore."

Suddenly, without warning, he continued, a giant hand would descend out of the dark frigid fog, plucking men off the decks of ships, tossing them into the sea, and in some cases, smashing the ships themselves to smithereens, dragging the unfortunate men down with it into the deep. It would stir up the water until it seethed and swirled until those not already drowned would be sucked down into the whirlpool.

With such hazards in mind, both real and fantastical, Tom decided to steer the ship out to sea. It was not a decision that pleased Robert.

"I must get to Donegal," Robert insisted

"Sure. And so you shall. And thank you, if you please, not as a drowned man."

Robert scowled, but could not argue.

The others cowered on the deck, wrapped in their cloaks, and tried as best they could to sleep or pass the time with dice or idle talk. It was in such an idle talk that Robert confided to his foster brother, Neill, a story Robert's foster mother had told him. When he was but two years old, she said, he had been very ill, and his foster parents thought he was like to die.

"They summoned an old man from nearby who knew the ways of the ancients and was skilled with herbs. He healed me where others had failed. But before he left he said, 'Mind he never goes to sea.' All he would say further to that was that if I did, no good would come of it."

Robert had tried to make light of the story, but Neill's expression showed he took it very seriously.

"T'is a *geis* he gave you," Neill said, a touch of awe in his voice. Neill had a long face. His upper teeth were large like a horse's, covered by an equally large upper lip. When he smiled, he was all smiles, but most of the time he just looked sullen. At the moment he looked as if Robert had just told him of a terrible calamity.

The Gaelic term made Robert pause. A *geis* was a taboo. A taboo that applied only to an individual, almost like a destiny. It was one of those superstitions of the pagan Irish that persisted despite centuries of Christianity.

"But you've gone to sea before have you not?" Neill said in a whisper, as if just voicing this thought was itself a forbidden thing.

Robert laughed, and shook his head, mocking Neill's seriousness. Neill, of course, was an Irish Irish. Robert, for all that his mother was Irish and he raised by Irish foster parents, and for all he considered himself truly Neill's brother, was still deep down a Norman, and he regarded the Irish superstitions skeptically.

"A man cannot live his life in fear of an old man's crypticism," was all he said. And I'll be damned, he might have added, that a superstition's going to stop me making the muster in Donegal. But he kept this to himself, wrapping himself in his cloak and going to sleep. Neill, on the other hand, lay awake, listening to the somber sloshing of the water against the clinker planking of the ship. Sometimes it would make a sickening sucking sound against the thick heavy water. It made Neill wish they had taken their chances in Thomond.

On the night of the third day they heard a sound like rain where there was no rain. It was the sound of bubbles rising to the surface from the sea. Presently the water began to boil, and many of the men feared some hideous monster was about to rise from the deep and swallow them, ship and all. But by the dawn the sea lay quiet again, and the fog began to lift, and by midday they found themselves under a clear blue sky.

And the sun shone upon them like a welcome friend, and a gentle breeze ruffled the limp sails so that they chaffed against the rigging and seemed to beckon them to make way.

And to the west, just upon the horizon, was an island....

"Ofttimes since," Sir Robert says to the Abbot, pausing briefly in his narrative, "I have wondered: was it all but an invention of my mind?"

Perhaps it was. The Abbot himself has suggested as much. Hanging there on the horizon like a mirage, the island seemed barely substantial. It appeared to float, and shimmered and fluttered like a banner in the breeze. Tom, too, at first dismissed it as a bank of clouds, and the others squinted and said they saw nothing, but Robert ordered that they set sail for it. Soon the water gurgled happily under the keel and the island began to grow bigger and as it did, the rest of the men, one after the other, saw it too.

Perhaps, suggests the Abbot, Robert had himself in some sense become enchanter to his men. Being himself under the grip of the spell, he had bewitched them into seeing and believing what was not there.

But it is also true, the Abbot continues, as if responding to some unspoken objection, that they could not have been enchanted had they not found in their own minds the material of enchantments, and built out of that, each and every one, his own island.

"Enchantments, like dreams, take place behind men's eyelids, and the mind itself is their accomplice, supplying all the raw material. Through closed eyes we see a world that is more vivid and real to us because the stuff of which it is made is the stuff of our very souls—the stuff of our yearning and longing."

3

Whatever the mechanism of spells, the truth was Robert and the rest of his retinue came to find themselves upon a beach. The land seemed to float beneath their feet (a fact they attributed to being at sea so long), the sky shone with an unreal shade of blue, and the sun beat down on them until their heads spun. But for that the land felt no different under their feet than any other land, though the trees and scrubs were strange to them, and they saw several birds they had never seen before with colorful plumes and unusual songs. Even Tom, who knew the seas all the way to Portugal, had never seen the like.

There was no sign of habitation—neither roads nor paths nor buildings. When they recovered their equilibrium they walked at least a mile inland through a wooded valley. They saw deer, who seemed to know no fear of man. MacErin removed his bow from its sheath and strung it in one movement, then picked an owl-quilled arrow and shot a young buck, all as easily as if he was as tying his shoes. They carried their prize back to the beach where they built a fire and, as night began to fall, roasted the meat on a spit.

Later, as the fire flared and flickered and sent sparks streaking into the dark, they heard loud noises like thunder. Many of the men were afraid, and wanted to return to the ship, but as the noise subsided, they grew calm.

"Better we spend the night here, sir," said Tom, poking the fire with a stick, "than another night out there, if you please."

He nodded towards the bay where the ship was anchored, and beyond that, the dark and silent sea. The men agreed. Anything was preferable to the cold hard deck of the ship, or the hold with its dank, stale air. Already they had made themselves comfortable, fashioning hollows in the sand by the fire and removing their swords and belts.

"The question is," put in the Irish named MacFael, "Where is here?"

Several voices concurred. It was a question on the tip of many tongues since the moment they had landed. Tom, on whom all eyes rested, looked at the circle of faces around the fire.

"The sea's not like the land. It hides what land reveals, and reveals what land keeps secret."

"And what may you be meaning by that?"

"That which I mean is, to put it simply, you ask the wrong question. You should ask not 'where' is here but 'what' is here."

"By the blood of God!" shouted the Norman, Reginald. "Words from you Irish are as clear as the fog in which we were three days lost. Pray your knowledge of the sea is better than your speech."

Robert laughed. Laughing was a means to set the Irish at their ease, for Reginald frequently showed little patience with the Irish, and they in turn regarded him suspiciously. The presence of a Norman in the kern was unusual, and a tricky thing to handle.

"One thing we know for sure—" Robert said. "—this is not Donegal."

Neill became suddenly agitated, pointing to Tom. "Tom says he thinks this island is enchanted."

It was the first occasion any of them had put in words what many of them had inwardly thought. Only Reginald sneered at the idea, and spat into the fire.

Tom nodded glumly, adding that if this were true they may well be trapped here forever. As usual he claimed to have heard many stories of such islands. The stories had it that those who landed upon such island never saw home again, but were lost forever. This was too much for Robert, who had the men's morale to think of.

"If that were true, my friend, you would not have heard the

stories of them, or be in a position to repeat them now, for if they were lost forever they could never have told their stories. Where's your logic, man?"

Tom considered this, but failed to see the point. He considered Robert rather cocky. How like the English, he thought, but held his tongue. There was little point in arguing with them, yet he could not resist.

"And what if they did return—not, to be sure, in their lifetimes, but, if you please, in the future and the present?"

"In the future and the present. What could you possibly mean?"

Sean knew what he meant. "He's thinking of Oisin."

"A legend. A fable."

"A legend recorded by the Saint himself. No idle fable. Tell him, Sean."

Sean's eyes flickered with the reflected light of the fire. He was, but for Neill, the youngest of the group, but of them all perhaps the most knowledgeable as far as legends and fables went.

"In our parish," he said, lowering his voice and forcing everyone to come closer, "not far from the church, there is an ancient ruin upon a hill. Nothing today but a mound of earth, but you can see it clear enough, the outline of a once great fort, and many people say they've seen the fairy folk there, or seen their effects. And so it was, many years ago, not in my grandfather's time, nor in his grandfather's time, but in his grandfather's grandfather's time, one All Saints Eve, that a man came, riding upon a stallion. A giant he was, over six foot tall, and dressed... you would not believe: attainment so magnificent, so glorious, like nothing you've ever seen. And he asked about the fort, and about those who had lived there, and where they were and what had happened, as if only yesterday he had departed, as if only yesterday those of whom he inquired had walked this earth.

"And when he was told that the fort had been ruins for centuries, that those who lived in it had long since turned to dust, their bones cradled in the clay and roots, he wept and lamented, so I've been told, and said what a fool he had been, what a fool to have lost everything because of the love of a woman. The woman he referred to was none other than the daughter of the king of the Land of Youth, and she came to him one morning while he was hunting with his brothers on the shore of the sea. A perfect picture of a morning it was too: the sea as still as could be, covered with a morning mist, the mist dissipating into the blue sky, the morning sun fast burning it away. Everything seeming to hang, ephemeral-like, as if in a perfect balance, like it would fall this way or that way, but never falling, just hanging and keepin' them breathless watchin' it hang. And as they watched she rode across the water, the hooves of her horse's silver shoes—for he was shod with silver, you see—flicking the tips of the waves, spattering water like it was dew from the grass. The drops flashed like jewels in the sun, they sang like the cords of a fine-strung harp, and fell in delicate patterns on the water.

"And how are you, sir, she said to one, and how are you, she said to another. She greeted all the company, but greeted him by name, him especially. To him she spoke of love. She spoke direct, made it known she would have him for a husband. No other would she accept, but only he. Thus she said. And sure she was fair, and sure her voice was sweet, and sure her eyes were entrancin', and it seemed to him the whole world hung still— aye, for the wind did not blow, the leaves on the trees did not stir, nor did the hounds bark or the horses neigh, and he could imagine nothing more intoxicating, nothing sweeter, nothing fairer, than to lie in her arms, feeling her touch, hearing her voice, looking into her eyes. And all other things of this world seemed as mere dross—unimportant, ridiculous, empty, the delusions of fools, compared to that.

"And not only love did she promise him; she promised him eternal youth as well, and happiness, and things we have no name for because they are beyond our normal ken, and though his brothers begged him not to go, and warned him that he was allowing himself to be bewitched, yet he heeded them not;

nor could they do anything to stop him, for a strange paralysis seemed to hold them in their place.

"She took him to her father's kingdom, which was located over the western seas on an island where trees forever blossomed, where the sun shone forever in a cloudless sky, and where the rivers ran with wine. No descriptions can do it justice, for the fairest things we can imagine are but a poor comparison to its bounty and pleasures."

Sean stopped, wet his whistle, then surveyed his audience to see how they were taking it in. He wanted to make sure they understood, and not being entirely satisfied they did, proceeded to add the very kinds of descriptions he had protested could never do it justice. He described how on this island one had only to desire drink, and it was provided—and not just in plenty but in cups that never emptied. Whatever food you desired, you had only to blink, and it appeared before you, prepared to perfection. On and on Sean went, offering examples. And when he saw they were all lapping it up, all nodding and saying to themselves what a wonderful place it must be, he let drop that it was, in fact, a perfectly boring place, and that the hero was, in fact, soon very miserable indeed. The point was... the thing about this island was... what you all must heed if the story is to make any sense or have any kind of moral... and there was a moral.... and the moral was... there was no gap, not even an infinitesimal one, between desire and its fulfillment. That was the problem. Desiring something and getting it were one and the same. You might not think this is a problem, Sean said. But it is. He asked his audience to imagine what this might be like for someone like the hero of this story, someone who, like Oisin, thrilled to the joy of the hunt, someone for whom the chase was the sport, and the kill merely the completion. Someone, he put it to them, unlike the weak, pathetic, self-serving, greedy and grasping people of the present world—like themselves, for example, for hadn't he had them all nodding with his descriptions, hadn't they all agreed that would be just grand. Someone rather like one of the heroes of Ireland's heroic past.

"Even pleasure has its limits for a hero, and a time comes when they no longer satisfy a noble mind and such a noble heart, when such a mind begins to question and such a noble heart begins to yearn for something else. So with time he grew homesick for his own country and for the company of those he had deserted, and whose voices he now recalled, begging him not to go. This time came after three years, or so it had seemed to him. His wife begged him to stay. 'Do not go,' she said, 'for I fear you will not return.' But now her words had no effect; her spell had worn out and now was powerless to keep him from his goal, as powerless as before his brother's words had been. Seeing she could not stop him she gave him a horse, the same she had ridden when she had first appeared to him, and instructed him carefully: whatever he did, he was not to dismount from his horse, his feet were not to touch the ground, not on any circumstances. He could ride wheresoever he wished, visit whom he wished, stay as long as he wished, so long as he obeyed these simple instructions.

"But she said nothing why this was so, nor warned him of what to expect when he came again into this world. She could not tell him that what to him had been but three years on her island had been three hundred in his world and that all those he loved and yearned to see again were long dead. To do so would be to admit that she had deceived him, and this she could not do. Let his eyes and ears do the telling, she reasoned. Better than for it to come from the same lips that had deceived him before.

"Imagine his surprise. Imagine his despair. As soon as he learned the truth, his dismay was so great that he could not help falling to the ground and weeping, clutching the grass, pounding the ground with his fist, watering the earth with his tears. Even as he did so, his hair turned to gray, his skin wrinkled up, his straight back bent, and within a minute he had turned to bones."

They had all listened with rapt attention. Now, suddenly, the silence took them by surprise. The flames flared and flickered and the men around the fire sighed and shook their heads. Meanwhile, Sean got out the harp he carried with him and plucked the strings casually for a while, then sang a melancholy but restful tune, weaving into it bits of the story he had just told.

> She came to him one morning
> While he was out a-hunting,
> On the shore of a lake
> Was he a-hunting.
>
> She rode across the water
> A-flicking drops like dew a-splattering,
> A-splattering.
> The drops they flashed like jewels,
> They sang like a fine strung harp.
> The drops they went a-splattering,
> A-splattering across the water
>
> The dogs they did not bark,
> Nor horses did they stir;
> The world hung in a balance,
> When the lady did appear.

And the fire flared and flickered and sent sparks streaked into the dark, and they made themselves hollows in the sand by the fire, and drew their cloaks about them.

In the morning they went in search of a source of fresh water, anxious not to lose any more time but to replenish their water and set sail that very day. They found a stream that ran to sea out of a wooded valley, and three men were sent back to the ship to fetch casks. After they had returned and were filling the barrels, a group of ten men approached.

They were all unarmed and elderly, dressed in long white robes like monks. One of the group stepped forward, hands outstretched, palm up in a gesture of peace, and greeted them. Speaking in an archaic dialect of Gaelic, he said his name was Sharlaugh, his voice trembling and cracking, though it was hard to tell if this were due to his old age or to his agitated state; he seemed quite excited. Robert had many questions: what island is this? What people live here? What were the strange noises we heard last night? Sharlaugh bade them follow him, saying only that all their questions would be answered and every need satisfied. Refusing hospitality could be unwise, so Robert agreed to follow.

They went up the same wooded valley they had come the day before. But whereas the previous day they had seen no signs of habitation, now they were amazed to find many. They traveled up a well-worn trail, past a glen with many cattle. Had they failed to observe this the preceding day? Or had it all appeared by magic? The Irish debated the issue as they walked, and after a short march they came to a prosperous estate. Here they saw more things to amaze them: well-tended fields of grain and pastures full of cattle and sheep, and houses, buildings and stables. There were many people about, all very busy, and in the center of all of this, on a hilltop, was a large manor house with a thatched roof, surrounded by a primitive stockade.

4

A great feast was prepared in their honor and they were entertained like princes. There was wine, ale, and mead; venison, hunks of bacon, stew simmered with leeks, and onions and turnips in a rich gravy; platters of mutton and poached salmon, plates of tripe and sweetbread; pies and bread and fruits, custards of berries and wheat cakes cooked in honey. For entertainment there were bards and acrobats and musicians.

Soon, intoxicated with wine, entranced by the entertainment, Robert forgot all their questions, which had before been so numerous, forgot even how they had come there, and from where they had come. Several times during the course of the evening he thought to himself that there was some question on his lips. But he could not recall what it was, and though several times it occurred to him that he had come there from far away, and after being lost in a fog, each time he dismissed this as but a shadow of a dream. He would take another long draught from his goblet and laugh to himself and try and carry on despite his confusion.

Beside him sat a beautiful woman. She seemed familiar. Her hair was dark—black as night—and her skin was fair and her eyes as blue as sapphires. She wore ruam on her lips, which gave them a lush red color. She was tall, as tall as he, and she wore a blue gown embroidered with fine yellow lace and secured around her neck by a gold broach. On her forearms, which were covered with a fine, silk-like hair, she wore gold bracelets in the shape of coiled snakes, and around her neck, a necklace with pearls and gold. An embroidered belt girded a slender waist, accentuating her hips and breasts, the contours of which the folds of the gown traced with intoxicating patterns.

Robert was wondering why she seemed so familiar when their eyes met. A rush of memories flooded into his mind. Her name was Una—"The One." He had been her lover, her suitor, and now—he was her husband. All this he had somehow forgotten, or so it seemed, then remembered, and remembering, it was as real as anything in his life had ever been real, so real everything else faded from his mind like a dream.

He recalled an entire life, a life in fact he'd never lived. He recalled every detail, though not all at once. Rather, they swirled in his mind like fragments. In one fragment he saw himself and Una by a waterfall. He knew without thinking about it that they and a party of men had come up into the hills in search of a stray bull. They had been separated from the rest of the group and sat on horseback and watched the waterfall in silence. Suddenly she turned and looked at him. She smiled a secret smile, as if he had whispered in her ear. But he had said nothing. He had only thought how beautiful she was. Like the waterfall—graceful, natural, majestic.

Then there were more fragments, many more fragments: of shared intimacies, of kisses, of caresses, of glances, of the sweat of lovemaking: all swirling in his mind like a flock of birds taking flight from a tree.

Another fragment: a shock of grief. He saw her face streaked with tears and panic. And he knew... he knew....

He shook his head. The wine. He didn't know. Didn't know anything. The world was full of wonders he only imagined, if at all.

His perplexed reveries were interrupted by Sharlaugh, the elder who had met them by the stream. Robert no longer recollected meeting Sharlaugh, however. Instead he fancied him to be someone else, or at least, a Sharlaugh he knew in different circumstances. For his part, Sharlaugh, having consumed a fair quantity of wine, now declared himself to be in the mood for song, and insisted there was no one in the world with a voice more fair than Princess Una. A handmaiden produced a beautiful harp, carved of oak and decorated with amber and abalone. Una took the instrument and went to the head of the

table where she took her seat and played a few chords to get the
tune, then sang in a beautiful crystal voice -

My heart is an island
Cast upon the sea;
Where flecks of moon and distant stars,
Wash upon the shore;
Singing your song.

The winter wind's a kiss
That's known the cold and deep;
The tide is a sensuous caress
That dies upon the sand -
A voice that whispers.

Clouds cast luminous sails,
Across the somber sky,
My thoughts ride the night until
The dawn drives night away
And I wake, alone.

Una's voice had a quality like pearls on velvet. The lyrical
melody of the ballad, as well as the song itself, evoked a most
powerful emotional response from the listeners. All sat frozen
in their seats, their eyes riveted, glistening in the torchlight.
Passions they had not previously known now rose up within
them like the tide of which Una sang. She sang of lost love,
of a lover gone over the sea, of emptiness and loneliness and
unspeakable depths of despair, but also of hope: hope for
deliverance, hope for redemption in love, in unqualified giving,
in waiting.

Still do I linger by
The shore, and venture
The portents of the sea
Will give some sign of thee.

I'll wait there til it does
I'll look in sea and sky
In wind, in waves, in stars,
Until you come to me.

When she had finished, the hall hung for several seconds in silence. Then the silence melted into a hum of voices, many calling for her to sing again. However, she returned her harp to her handmaiden's care and the other musicians struck up a more lively note while she made her way towards her seat.

She did not sit down, however, but only paused briefly beside Robert, lowering her eyes and then disappearing. Something passed between them. He sensed she wanted him to follow her and thought he ought to excuse himself to the others. But the others were all very much preoccupied themselves, some with other maidens, some with the music, some with the wine. Seeing this he slipped away without a word.

Outside the hall he found himself in a cold and drafty corridor. There was no sign of Una, but as he proceeded down the corridor he sensed his way without thinking, as if he were in a familiar place, and always, though he did not see her he felt her presence leading him on. Up a long flight of stairs, a window awarded a view of a half-moon hanging over a silhouette of poplars rustling in the night breeze and in the distance the sea shimmered, reminding him of Una's song. Somewhere behind the silhouette of trees, he knew, a ship lay anchored, but he did not know how he knew this, or what it meant.

Eventually he came to a half-closed door the other side of which was the warm glow of a fire. He entered, and saw Una.

She had removed her embroidered belt and the golden broach which bound her gown around her neck and deftly slipped the straps over her shoulder so the gown slid silently to the floor. There she stood, proud in her nakedness, clad only in the gleaming jewelry around her neck and on her forearms, the flickering glow from the fire dancing over her milk-white skin, lending it the shade of passion.

He approached her, as if spellbound. Her head tilted back

and her lips parted, anticipating his embrace. He lifted the long locks of dark hair that draped over her shoulders and she fell into his arms, pulling at his clothes. The strength and force of her passion surprised him. She bit his ear and lips, and scratched his back, ran her tongue over his body, and writhed and rubbed against him. She seemed to be trying to get out of herself, as if she were undergoing some sort of transformation, physical metamorphosis. He thought for a minute she was possessed and would lose herself in madness. Her skin burned like a hot iron.

An erratic dance led them in a pattern of zigzags to the bed, where they lingered, teetering on the edge. Like cannibals they feasted on each other. Giving and taking became a single act, swirling in a maelstrom in the center of which their passion alone existed. He thought the room dissolved... they were in a forest... out of the corner of his eyes he thought he saw woods, brush, creatures, owls which looked at him with round, yellow eyes... deer... beyond the forest, the sea... he heard the surf, resonating in his ears, almost inside his head.

But he did not stop to either confirm or deny these bizarre perceptions. Gently now, he pulled her down onto the bed. She flung her head back and moaned, and in her eyes, which she opened only a thin slit, the fire danced and glowed, and tears rose up and ran down her cheeks. He licked the tears with his tongue. Her moans changed to sobs, and her sobs to a sigh and finally she lay still; her arms, limp, slid off his back. As if it were fed by her own passion the fire in the hearth subsided.

The light of the moon and the stars that shone through the open window now cast a bluish tinge upon her milky skin, which was covered in beads of sweat. The night air that whispered over them caused her to shiver, and she drew the covers over her. She rolled onto her side facing him and for a while played with the lobe of his ear, saying nothing. Then she fell off to sleep, exhausted.

Robert lay on his back, staring up at the underside of the thatched roof which he had stared at, he thought, countless times before, but which now seemed strangely different. Just beyond the wall he could hear shouting and merrymaking. As Una slept he slipped out of bed, careful not to wake her, and followed the sound. It came from behind a heavy, embroidered tapestry. Drawing a corner of this aside he discovered that the room in which they were sleeping was a loft that looked out over the great hall. But of course he had known that.

Below a group of strangers, oddly familiar, were at the end of a feast. Some of them were making ready for bed. He could not recall who they were or what they were doing there, then recollected they had come by sea, having lost themselves in a dense fog. But he did not make any connection between himself and them. When he thought of it, his head spun. Too much wine, he thought, and returned to bed. Una awaited him there. How fortunate he was to have her, he thought, kissing the back of her neck where the fine hair at the nape caught the moonlight. He reflected back on their life together. How many years had it been? Strange he could not remember.

"Donegal," he muttered out loud to himself.

What did it mean: "Donegal"?

He fell asleep.

5

The Abbot looks up, his old eyes shining in the darkness. He draws in his breath, and Sir Robert stops his narrative, waiting to hear what he has to say.

"You ascribed your confusion to too much wine?"

"Yes."

"Could the wine, perhaps, have been drugged?"

"I have no experience with such drugs."

"Nor I. We had a brother in the abbey, though, an herbalist, who knew much about such things—drugs that can bend the mind, that can rouse unheard of passions and lusts, that can trap demons and open the doors to Heaven and Hell (though a man can never be certain which door will be opened to him). He might have thrown some light upon this matter. However, he died only a short time ago, may God rest his soul."

He crosses himself and hangs his head in silence for a moment. The brother had been dear to him.

"You said that just prior to this rush of so-called memories you thought at first you recognized this woman. She reminded you of someone else, perhaps?"

"She did not remind me of anyone. She was herself. It was more as if I'd seen her in a dream."

"This is what you believe?"

"Not what I believe. It's an impression. She seemed to sense the same thing about me."

"How so?"

"The way she looked at me. There was a flicker of recognition, then a sort of accepting."

"Who then did she think you were?"

"*Myself, Father.*"

"*Then, perhaps, she had seen your coming in a dream. Perhaps this was the meaning of her song. Or perhaps she had divined it by some magical means. Was she then, an enchantress?*"

"*Not an enchantress, Father, but enchanted.*"

The Abbot looks at him with the dark dubious air only one of his age and position can summon.

"*I wonder, my son, if you are fully qualified to distinguish between the two.*"

The vehemence of his words surprises Sir Robert. To tell him more about the effect Una had upon him would only serve to convince the Abbot that she was a witch. Perhaps that is his opinion of all woman.

"*I can only tell you what I experienced, and the thoughts that came to me at the time. Also there is more, which I have yet to tell.*"

The Abbot looks at Sir Robert with a troubled eye, fidgeting with his bony white fingers impatiently.

"*The thoughts that come to one on such occasions may well lead one astray. They become mixed up with our passions, and with vice.*"

"*For that, Father,*" *Sir Robert says, somewhat impatiently, "I have already done penance.*"

The Abbot blinks. He had forgotten. This is not a confession. Something made him speak harshly without his even thinking. Something inside him—an emotion he has not felt for years. Was it envy? Envy for this man's sexual gratification? No. The Abbot had conquered lust long ago. The envy he feels is for something else. Because this man has gone where the Abbot has secretly longed to go himself. This man has not stood upon the cliffs of Innismane, has not ached within his heart at the sight of what he knows to be unattainable, has not spent a lifetime studying ancient tomes and charts, collecting the tales of fishermen and sailors, bits of driftwood. This man simply slipped through a fog while sailing from Kerry to Donegal and entered a world that had been denied the most ardent dreamer.

"*Of course,*" *he says, overcoming his reaction. "Please go on. What happened next?*"

6

In the early morning light she watched him sleeping. His eyes flickered behind his lids. She had waited for him to wake, wondering what color his eyes were. A simple thing. She had not noticed before. Though the Matrix could weave multilayers of illusions it could not fill in the details her passion had shunned to note. The Matrix painted with a broad brush, deceiving the mind with the force and depth of emotion and conviction, but letting details trickle like water through a sieve—a phenomenon that accounted for the always empty feeling she and all the people of the island lived with all their lives.

Who was this man who had come as if from nowhere, shattering the timeless tedium of her island? From his features she guessed he was not of her race. Nor was he one of the invading Gaels who had brought war and chaos to her land and people. She wondered what had happened to her people—those who had not, like her, been banished, frozen out of time. Had they all been killed, enslaved, driven from their lands?

Who was this man, bringing with him desires and hopes she had thought were long dead within her? She was not sure she wanted these desires and hopes reawakened. She was afraid it would only bring her pain and disappointment. Yet she could not deny what she had felt the night before. She had clung to him as if afraid to let go, fearing he was not, could not, be real, yet knowing he was, and must be, real.

"Real." The word itself made her shudder.

Sharlaugh had said it would happen eventually. No spell was perfect, and the Matrix always inclined towards unity. Like a stone balanced on another stone. There were stones that remained like this for centuries. For millennia. But nature dictated that one day they would fall.

She was a stone balanced on another stone. There was no telling how long she would remain. A hundred years. A thousand years. A million years. It was like throwing a dice. It depended on probabilities.

Could that mean she had already been a million years in enchantment? It was impossible to say. She had no sense of time here. She had no way to be certain of anything. It was fine for Sharlaugh to speak of probabilities. Probabilities gave no certainty. Certainties knew no probability. It could have been a million. It could have been only one. Either was possible, but that did not make it real. The probabilities of either varied, depended on factors. The factors themselves depended on probabilities.

Sharlaugh could talk endlessly about factors and probabilities. He had only speculation. Like her, he'd had plenty of time to speculate on what had happened, and she respected his wisdom and knowledge. Yet it all seemed pointless, empty. It didn't end in answers, only more questions.

Just then her lover stirred, his eyelids flickering, then opening. They were, she noted, green like the water of a jade bearing stream. They fixed immediately upon her, and he smiled. Then they shifted, aimlessly, as if trying to focus on something in the air. He seemed to search the air; then, as if his eyes had found an invisible point of reference, his face lit up.

"I had a dream," he said.

"Tell me," she prompted.

"In my dream I was lost in a dense fog on the sea. When the vapors lifted there was an island. Landing on the island I could no longer remember from where I had come. I met a beautiful maiden. The maiden was yourself, Una, but I did not at first recognize you. Then...."

He got no further than this. Suddenly he sat up, looking around in a daze, running his hand through his hair, stuttering and blubbering. A cool breeze blew through the window, ruffling the curtains, and outside the window the birds were singing. He regarded the window as if it were an apparition.

His disorientation was understandable. The enchantment had that effect. It altered memory, flooded the mind, rearranged perception.

"Where am I?" he demanded. His voice was tinged with suspicion, and his eyes frightened her. "What island is this?"

"You'd better get dressed," she said, throwing him his clothes.

On the west side of the island there was a sheer cliff that dropped into the sea, and on the other side a more gentle, sometimes rugged, slope. In this direction you could see the manor house from which they had come, pastures and woodland, even, far in the distance, a ship, the *Black Sligo* anchored in a bay. Beyond, on all sides — the sea.

As far as one could see there was the sea.

"This is our island." She gestured with her hand to include all three-hundred-and-sixty degrees. "As you can see, we are alone. In a sense, there is not much point in asking what island this is. That would suggest that this island stands in some relation to the rest of the world, such that it requires a name to distinguish it from other islands. That is not the case, I am afraid to say. This island is simply — the island. For us, there is no other."

He was about to tell her that what she was saying was absurd then she blurted out quite suddenly, "From here, though, I once saw islands in the distance."

A brisk wind was blowing and blew so strong that it caused her crimson dress to flutter like a banner, clinging to her body like flames. Last night she had worn blue. He recalled last night her body seemed to take on the colors of the fire and of the night alternately. He watched her, intrigued, as she faced into the gale and breathed deeply, her eyes closed, a raptured smile on her lips as if the gusts were the hands of a lover, caressing her. He felt a tinge of jealousy and remembered the song she had sung at the banquet. Was this her lover, speaking to her through the wind? The lover lost to the sea? But he sensed it was not so. He was the lover. He did not know how he knew this. But he knew it.

"As clear as day I saw them—islands. Others have seen them too. Here on the island, almost everyone has, at one time or another, seen the islands to the west."

"They tell the same stories where I come from." He was curt, impatient for answers. She ignored his comment, let the wind take it beyond hearing.

"Some say if one had a ship, and if one could sail there, one would find people like ourselves."

She turned and looked into his eyes, trying to make some contact with his mind. *If one had a ship.... You have a ship.*

"...One would find people there... people who like us gaze westward and see upon the horizon islands like their own, people like themselves, people who gaze westward and see upon the horizon islands like their own..."

She pulled a strand of hair out of her mouth that the wind had blown.

"Islands like their own, people like themselves, people who gaze to sea..."

She sighed and a look of extreme pathos came over her.

"Why do you tell me this?"

She looked at him sharply: "Don't you understand? This island is one of those."

"What do you mean?" he asked, though his eyes revealed that already the answer was haunting him.

"I mean," she said, and at that moment a cloud passed over the sun and dark shadows skirted over the hills and cliffs, "this island is enchanted."

The look in his face told her she had got his attention. His eyes darted from her, to the ground, to the sky, to the sea, as if he were putting them all in place inside his head.

"And some say this is all there is, and one could sail forever and find always the same thing, a great circle of emptiness, of gazing out to sea, of chasing illusions, of yearning and imagining. And there is no end to it. It is as if the islands were two mirrors set against each other, generating an infinity of images, an endless sequence of illusions. And this island is only one in this endless sequence — an endless sequence embedded on a vast matrix, a Matrix of Enchantment."

The events he had experienced so far were strange enough to suggest that more things were possible in this world than he had hitherto believed. But he could not think of anything to say.

"But others say it is just illusion, and like a mirror it can be shattered.

She examined him closely, as if trying to decide if he was an illusion himself. Then she said abruptly, "You are not Danaan. You are not Gael. What race are you, and what brings you here?"

It seemed to surprise him that she had questions of her own. It caused him to look at her more sympathetically. He had assumed he was the one who was lost, the one vulnerable.

"Danaan?"

"That is my people."

"I know nothing of Danaans. But you are right I am not a Gael, though my foster father was. I am of the 'middle nation.'"

"Middle nation?"

"Neither Irish nor English."

"I know nothing of 'English.'"

"We English came in King Henry's time. The Second, not the Third. But many things have happened since, and some of us no longer...."

Robert searched for words. Should he say, "No longer are loyal to the English king"? It was the king who had betrayed them. Left them to fend for themselves, then condemned them for doing just that.

"We fight together with the Irish, but we are not Irish, or only half so."

He explained how his mother was Irish, and how he

had been raised by Irish foster parents in deference to Irish customs.

"Many things have happened," Una said simply. "I fear I am completely out of my time."

"And I of mine, for as to what brings me here, it is just as I told you this morning, for that was no dream, but the truth. And as I came, so must I leave, and as soon as possible, I fear. For I must be in Donegal to make the muster."

"You are to war, then?"

He nodded.

"I thought as much. Your men have that look."

Una, with a last glance to the west, turned on her heels and led the way down the path by which they had come.

"I know nothing of your 'English.' But if your foster father was a Gael, surely he told you of the Tuatha De Danaan. Or has so much time passed that we are completely forgotten now?"

"What you speak of, I think, are legends and fables."

"Is it so, then?"

"What?"

"Are my people but legends and fables to you?"

"Well, I will not say. I've heard my share of fables, but never paid much heed. But I will say if you know nothing of English, then you know nothing of the world."

"That may be. This island is not part of the world as you know it."

The path they had been following led them down a wooded gully. Robert, curious about the way she had described the enchantment as the "Matrix," asked her to explain.

"The Matrix is more than just enchantment. In fact, to call it such may be a misnomer. The enchantment is really a distortion of the Matrix. You can think of the Matrix as if it were a fabric, as it is, in fact: the fabric of space and time itself. Then enchantments are akin to a heavy stone thrown upon the fabric that draws the fabric down, forming a hollow, almost a hole, in the fabric."

Robert struggled to follow the strange concepts he was hearing from her lips. He was a practical man, trained in the brutal art of war, anesthetized to most other aspects of life. Yet, he resisted the impulse to dismiss what she was saying as nonsense. He wanted to understand, and to do so he was prepared to consider things he might not previously have thought worthy of consideration by a man such as himself.

"The Matrix," Una continued, seeing she had a willing listener, "is a web woven over the whole world. There is more than one level to the Matrix, as there is in a weaving. There are strands and threads, warps and woofs. Everything without exception is in some way tied to the Matrix, but most men remain bound by the ties they are born with. They never move from one strand to another, let alone from one level to another."

The description could well apply to himself, he reflected. At least until this moment.

"My people learned to use the Matrix to move from one level to another. They learned to combine levels and create combinations that made worlds within worlds. They used this sometimes to escape their enemies. They made themselves invisible, disappeared into the air, or into the ground. Then they reappeared at will, to make an—ambush—" she made a playful gesture as if ambushing him herself— "or cause mischief."

Robert recalled stories his mother had told him of "the little people." If that is what Una meant, he mused: She herself was by no means little. Almost as tall as himself, in fact.

"Some had greater power than others. They became leaders and shamans. And of these, some abused their power. They cast evil spells. Among the evil spells they cast was the spell of 'banishment.' In this spell the Matrix was used to weave a web from which the victim could not escape. The victim was effectively imprisoned for all time."

Unexpectedly Robert found they had returned to the manor house, coming upon it from the rear.

"You, I take it, are such a victim."

"To my misfortune, yes," she replied, and led him through a small door at the back into the great hall, "though not for long.

But we will speak more of this later. Your men are waiting for you by the hearth. I shall see to the day's preparations."

7

A bronze cauldron had been filled with wine and meat and herbs and was now simmering on the fire. Robert's companions had gathered around. Someone had provided them with ale and there was a great commotion among them, for like Robert they had all had similar experiences of forgetting and remembering, and they were arguing among themselves whether they had dreamed it all or if it had been real.

"Did I not say this place is enchanted?" said Tom, scratching his beard and grinning, responding to something MacFael had just finished saying that Robert had not heard. "And sure it is too."

"And were you not also saying we'd ne'er be leaving it?" put in MacFael, his tone a verbal sneer. "Why then should you be grinnin' so. T'is you that brung us here. You should na' steered us out to sea but kept us to the land."

"Sure—and have us wrecked upon the rocks in the fog? Upon my word, you know naught of ships and sea."

MacFael gave him a cold stare laced with contempt, but evidently thought the pilot unworthy of more eloquent attention.

"What's the hurry to leave?" said Reginald, taking a long draught of ale. He'd listened to the exchange between MacFael and Tom with wry amusement, as was his tendency whenever Gaels were concerned, but especially when they quarreled. "We've everything we need here, and more."

Robert listened to all of this from where he stood by the back door. None had seen him there until the moment he stepped out of the shadow, impatient with the direction their talk had taken them.

"Have you forgotten we have promises to keep in Donegal, lads?"

Neill, who had been sitting with his back to Robert, not participating in any of the conversation, jumped up and ran to Robert, throwing his arms around him.

"Where have you been?" he demanded.

The poor boy, Robert reflected, was still so much dependent on him, almost childish. He would have to learn to be less so, if he were to become a man.

Sean said, "We've been waiting for you to show up. What have you discovered about..." his vocabulary grew suddenly short "...all of this?"

"'All of this?'" Robert came closer to the fireside. Someone placed an ale glass in his hand, and he took a swig. It tasted pleasantly of fennel and caraway. Then he began to tell them as best he could all that Una had told him, though considerably less eloquently and not very clearly. They understood little of his description of the Matrix, which he described as a "blanket" rather than a "fabric." However, when he described to them the islands to the west Una had told him about (leaving off the part about the mirrors) they became quite interested. All of them had heard such stories too, and Reginald claimed to have heard that such islands were paved with gold.

Tom, who was still in a sour state of mind, gave a dismissive grunt. "There be hundreds of such stories," he said, testily. "Even charts. Men who claim to have been there. Aye, and come back, if it please you, sir, to keep things neat and logic-like."

He nodded at Robert, recalling Robert's rebuke the night they landed and sat around the fire.

"Full of stories, too. Gold and fabulous riches. What-have-you. One story's as good as another, I say. Take 'em as they are, or don't take 'em at all."

"God's toenails!" shouted Reginald, exploding in a rage. "If you don't hold your tongue I'll cut it out!"

Reginald in a rage was a frightening thing to behold. His face turned red, a vein in his forehead bulged, and the short black hairs on his bullish neck stood out like the prickles on a porcupine. Tom, his mouth agape, thought better of saying anything.

A silence fell over the group. The fire crackled and hissed and somehow spoke their thoughts. Tom, seeing Reginald's complexion turn from red back to pink and brown, pulled his leathery ear and grinned sheepishly in an imitation of subservience designed to placate Reginald's tyrannical temper.

"Reginald's got some tales of his own," explained Sean.

"Yes, well, I've done my share of traveling. You hear all sorts of things traveling: people who've been places, seen places, or heard things about places, islands with cities, all with fabulous buildings crowned with golden domes and silver towers. Places with so much gold and so many gems that the inhabitants treat gold like dirt, precious gems like garbage; they swept them into the gutter, and a man can take all he wants for himself, no one would stop him or give a damn."

"What then did they use for money?"

"Money?"

"Yes. If they didn't use gold, what used they in its stead? Men everywhere use something for money, otherwise they can't trade, can't save up treasure, can't become rich."

"Well, I have no idea. What does it matter?"

"Well, it reminds me of a story I heard, a story told by a merchant shipwrecked on just such an island while returning from the continent."

"Does it? And what, since you bring it up, did the people on this island use for money?"

"Nuts."

"Nuts?"

"Not just any nut. What they used for money was a particular kind of nut, something like a walnut, which had a peculiar quality, for if a person possessed the nut the nut would, in time, absorb the quality of virtue of its possessor; the possessor could imbue the nut with his virtue. Only then did the nut become valuable."

"Ptah! That's absurd. I've never heard such a crazy story. You mean, all they had to do was pick a nut off a tree, imbue it with... virtue... and go on a spending spree?"

"In essence, that's the idea. Of course, it depended on your virtue, on how many good deeds you'd done. You could only imbue as many nuts as you have virtue."

"What? Only one nut for every good deed?"

"Something like that. And for scoundrels and villains it worked the other way. If someone gave them a nut imbued with virtue, it instantly lost its virtue and became worthless."

"Blood of Christ! That'd make paupers out of most men. In fact, I'd wager there were not many rich men on this island."

"On the contrary. The effect of such a means of exchange was to make all men, but habit, virtuous, for villainy profited them nothing, and men, if they can't profit from thievery and deception, will soon give it up. No villain or scoundrel on this island ever became wealthy; all were condemned to the lowest classes of society, as they justly deserved, while virtuous men everywhere became wealthy and rose to the top of society as naturally as oil rises to the top of water. And, since virtue was inevitably rewarded, and villainy punished, the population of the island grew virtuous. A more virtuous population could not be imagined."

"Rot! Villainy is in men's nature. Has been since Eve picked the apple."

"But men have free will. Men can chose good, and will chose good if good is rewarded, and turn away from evil if evil is not rewarded."

"Ha! Only in a place where men use nuts for money!"

There was a chorus of laughter at this, and Reginald, beaming with delight at having scored a point are Sean's expense, took a long draught of his spiced ale.

"But tell us," asked Neill, "What happened to the merchant in your story?"

"Well, the system used by the islanders for the acquisition of wealth posed a bit of a problem for him. For the truth was, he was a rogue and a villain; he just didn't have the 'talent,' as he put it, to imbue the nuts with value, or to sustain the value of nuts he acquired. He learned, of course, that if he acquired the nuts by his own hard work, and honestly and honorably, that the nuts tended to hold their value... at least, according to the natives; he himself could not distinguish one nut from another. But he did not much relish hard work and on the whole preferred earning his living by devious means, so soon found that he was condemned to poverty and to the charity of the inhabitants, and all this while surrounded by gold and precious gems. So naturally he began to look for ways to return to his own country, preferably with as much gold and as many gems as he could carry. The islanders, realizing that he was not much good to them, helped him on his way, giving him a boat and providing it with all he needed for a voyage. They were puzzled by the sacks and sacks of gold and precious gems he loaded in his boat, but offered no objections. In this way he returned to his own country a rich man, and, of course, given the nature of society in this world, he became a powerful and respected man."

Robert looks up, surprised to hear the Abbot laughing. He laughs in short, wheezy spurts, a broad grin exposing a single tooth on his upper gum. There is scorn and derision in his laughter.

"A Pelagian! A Pelagian!" he wheezes.

"Father?"

"Your harpist friend is a heretic."

"How so?"

"He believes that men can achieve salvation by the simple exercise of free will, by cultivating good habits, by storing up good deeds as a squirrel stores up nuts for winter. Then what use would men have for the Church? What use for the holy sacrament?"

Robert has to admit he had not thought of this. The Abbot becomes suddenly serious.

"Then think of this: if men do good only to earn nuts, or points in heaven, or what have you, then the possibility of any self-less deed is denied, is it not? Every good deed become spiritually meaningless. Does it not?"

Robert thinks hard, but can only say, "How so?"

"Because every good deed is no more than a selfish grab for nuts, and avoiding evil is pure calculation."

"*But surely that is God's will. For what is the promise of heaven or the fear of hell but a goad to men's wills? To make men good.*"

"*Make men good? Baa! Burn heaven! Burn it to cinders! Throw water on the fires of hell! Put them out forever! God has no time for men's fear or desires. He'd rather see a man rapacious in pursuit of gold than acting like a busy squirrel counting up virtue like nuts. What God wants, is to see a man, one man, any man, do good simply because it is good, the way Job did. For Job, a virtuous man, lost everything, wealth, health, family, yet never lost his faith, never wavered in his virtue. Do you think you can do the same?*"

Robert does not have to think hard. In fact, despite his love for Lady Una, which he never questions himself and which he would permit no man to question, he nevertheless has to admit that he never stopped calculating his own advantage.

8

The rest of the morning they spent in a more subdued manner without incident, quietly getting drunk. Servants came and began spreading sweet flag, meadowsweet and woodruff over the rushes on the floor. Then they sprinkled water perfumed with aromatic herbs over that so that the room began to smell as fresh as a mountain meadow in the spring. MacErin went for a walk and came back with shafts for arrows, which he proceeded to prepare. Reginald polished his broadsword. Sean strummed his harp, sang bits and pieces of songs, but none to the end. Towards noon Una returned, having changed into a black dress, with a necklace and bracelets of jet. With her raven-black hair and black dress her sapphire-blue eyes and ruby-red lips looked like jewels set on alabaster, and seeing her Robert thought she was even more beautiful than before. It came to him suddenly that he loved her in a way he had not loved any other woman, and certainly in a way he did not, could not, love his wife, Maire, who now seemed to him plain and simple. He could no more consider leaving and returning to Ireland without her than he could consider cutting off his own arm.

But he did not have time to brood on this too long. The servants, acting on directions from Una, began to stir the stew and prepare dishes for serving. Musicians, playing reed pipes and strings, began to fill the air with a Babel of different melodies, tuning their instruments and testing their repertoire. Tankards of wine and ale were being carried to the table in preparation, it seemed, not merely for a continuation of the previous night's revelry, but for an escalation.

Presently Una invited them all to sit, and saw to it each was served. She promised to tell them everything, but only once they had eaten, and only once her obligations as a hostess were completely fulfilled.

"I shall not be a niggardly hostess, and so do not be niggardly guests. For every cup I fill, let me see an empty one to be filled. And no sipping like women, or I myself will set the pace and let *you* keep up with *me*. I have a tale to tell, but I will not tell it unless you are drunk. It's a fantastic tale, and sober men have no imagination for the fantastic."

There were great cheers and approval for this plan, though it took the better part of the afternoon before Una was satisfied the required amounts of drink had been consumed. Many times they urged her to speak, only to have her defer until such time as they were well prepared and their imaginations suitably lubricated.

It was an incredible and strange tale she told them when finally they met the precondition, a tale of misbegotten love, broken promises, vengeance and magic—how the island came to be the way it was and how she came to be the prisoner of a perverse enchantment. It happened long ago. How long ago she could not say, for here on the island time had little meaning, though she surmised from the things Robert had told her that at least a thousand years had passed.

"Only suspend for now your everyday conceptions," she said. "Assume everything is possible, that ideas can transmute form, that mind has infinite power over matter, that love and hate are stronger than life and death, that the very ground upon which we stand itself rests only in our conception of it."

Their rapt expressions suggested they had no problem with this. So prefaced her narrative began: This island, she said, was no island at all, nor had it been, nor should it be. It existed neither by the will of God nor cause of nature, but only by the most foul malice and sorcery. Previously it had been a part of the mainland of Ireland, known to her people as "Dana's land." It formed the principal lands of her father, a great Danaan chief.

Her father had a notion to ally himself with a powerful

chieftain by the name of Danal MacFinn, a man who had, among other things, managed to steal the secret knowledge of the Danaan holy men, and who thus had acquired considerable power. He had a great knowledge of the Matrix. He could touch it with his mind—no mean feat, Una said. To seal the alliance Una's father had offered his daughter in marriage to MacFinn.

"That—'honor'—was meant for my elder sister, but before the wedding could take place my sister fell off her horse and broke her neck. I, who had different plans, suddenly found myself taking her place.

"Now, MacFinn was an ugly and brutish man. He was short, hairy and misshapen, with droopy eyelids and dark, pockmarked skin."

Una embellished this description with gestures and parody so that they could almost see MacFinn standing before them.

"But it wasn't just his appearance that made him revolting. That, in fact, was but the outward reflection of a darker fault within—a misshapen soul, a blemished character, a deficiency of feeling and decency. He was the most selfish, cruel and avaricious man you will ever meet, and if you never met him—count yourself blessed.

"Naturally, I wished nothing to do with him. As the time of the wedding approached I begged my father to break his promise. At first he refused, aware of the dire consequences that would inevitably follow, consequences I had no appreciation of myself. I was young and strong-willed and self-centered, and I vowed I would cut off MacFinn's head with a dagger, and cut out his heart and eat it on the wedding night if my father forced me to marry MacFinn."

She said this with such vehemence (and for emphasis drove the knife she had been using to eat with into the table) that there was none present who doubted she was capable of carrying out the deed and would have done just what she said.

"My father finally relented and broke off the engagement. MacFinn was enraged. He gnashed his teeth, stamped his feet and finally threw himself on the ground in a frenzy. And, of course, he refused to return my sister's dowry, which had already been put in his trust in anticipation of the wedding, a dowry that should have been mine. Among the items of this humble treasure was a large gem the size of a chestnut and the color of the sea. Because of its unusual hue it was known as 'the Stone of Lir' (Lir being the god of the sea). It was a family heirloom, passed down from my mother who died when I was still a child, after a sudden illness. She had the jewel from her father, a man, I regret, I never knew, for my mother was not a native of the land of Dana, but came from far away.

"The stone was reputed to have great magical power. Indeed, there are so many powers attributed to it one can't imagine them all. Some of them go beyond our ability to conceive and so can't be spoken. Nor would I speak of them now but that they pertain to my story, and if my story seems unbelievable, then it is because the powers of the stone are unbelievable."

Una paused, her voice growing hoarse, and took a sip of wine. Then she regarded the faces all turned towards her up and down the table, every one of them silent, many of them acting on her cue and drinking from their cups.

"MacFinn, who as I said had stolen the knowledge of the Danaan holy men, knew how to use the power of the stone and he used the stone now to take revenge for his wounded pride and lust. First, he caused a distortion in the Matrix. Then with one great stroke of his staff, and with many incantations for effect, he severed this piece of land, which before had been part of the mainland, and relocated it far to sea."

A look of great sadness passed briefly over her face, then her jaw set firmly and her eyes flashed. When she spoke next her voice cracked with anger.

"My father, who had seen what MacFinn was up to and who had ridden out with a dozen of his best men to stop him, rode into an abyss as a great chasm opened under his feet and the sea poured in between."

She paused, getting control over her feelings.

"Then, again using the Stone of Lir, which he left here on the island to ensure the spell lasted forever and never wore out, he laid upon this island, already cast far out to sea, the following enchantment: that it be but a phantom to the eyes of mortal men; that should it be seen, should not be approached; that should it be approached, should appear to disappear like a mirage so that no man should ever land upon its shores; finally, that should any of the inhabitants attempt to escape and return to the real world from which they came, the opposite should hold true, and even as they should seem to leave the island behind, even should it drop beneath the horizon, even so should it appear again in front of them, and should they appear to be sailing in circles, and they should never leave."

Again Una used the analogy of a heavy weight cast on a taunt fabric making a distortion, or dent, in the otherwise smooth plane. She described how a marble, rolled upon the surface of the fabric, would be drawn into the distortion. This was the effect for the inhabitants of the island, for even as they believed themselves to be sailing away, and the island receding behind them, so the island would appear again in front of them, as if they were sailing in circles, and they could never escape, try as they might.

For those outside the spell worked in reverse, as if the marble, instead of making an indentation, pulled up the fabric. A ship sailing toward the island would be repelled, so that even though the ship appeared to those on board to be sailing forward instead it would be retreating from the island.

"So did the enchantment banish us, every man, woman and child of us, from all mankind. Also, from time."

The latter statement caused many to pause and set down their cups, and Una, rising to her feet, strode down the table, looking every man in the eye as she passed him.

"Now to be banished from man is one thing, but to be banished from time — this is an unspeakable thing, and difficult to explain in words. Let me just say that time is not of the same nature on this island as it is outside. Outside, time passes; on our island, time hangs suspended like a ship becalmed. Only the illusion of time persists. Days appear to pass. Interminable. Day upon day until the mind bends under the weight of days passed, piling one upon the other on an already over-burdened memory until one wishes only to forget, to start again, only one cannot. Here there are no true accomplishments to achieve, no joy in pleasures, no challenge to living; one simply goes on, day after day, days empty of significance, without direction—an endless, empty present without any future, and with a past that is more the stuff of dreams than of reality.

"But no matter how many days pass, no matter how many years of days elapse on the outside, people here age not a day. Guess, if you will, my age. But do not let appearances deceive you. I tell you by your time I am a thousand years old—at the very least. And I lived every day of it! But not a day of it like any day you've ever lived. For not a day of it had a beginning or an end, and not a day of it had either a tomorrow or a yesterday. Think of it, if you can. But do not think too much or you will despair. As we despair. Wishing nothing but to grow old and die, we remain as we are, frozen in time, condemned to our island, apparently for all eternity."

Those who only hours before had seemed so willing to spend their lives in feasting and drinking, believing they had all the time in the world, now reflected what a mistake this would have been, and what a price they would have paid for their pleasure, exchanging all meaning and significance for empty entertainment. Robert, however, emboldened with liquor, far from letting her story dampen his spirits, was busy unraveling it in his mind, and he thought he saw a flaw in it, which he did not hesitate to point out.

"What about us? We are here, are we not, but should not be. If what you say is true we should have... rolled off the blanket or something like that."

The others laughed, and Una smiled, for the first time in her narrative her eyes flashed with something besides anger and hate.

"No spell, even one as great as this, is without some weakness, some—'chink,' if you will—though which it may 'leak,' or through which things may pass, as you passed. So we—occasionally—will find bits of driftwood on the beach, driftwood that could only have come from the outside world. How it gets here is just a matter of chance, and chance is just a matter of time, they say, and probabilities, for given enough time, all chances occur. Sooner or later. And sooner or later someone, some person and not just a piece of driftwood, was bound to find the chink, without the least intent or plan, and sail through. And then..."

"And then?"

"Tell me, what did you do upon landing?"

"What? Well, we scouted around, found no signs of habitation, killed a deer, lit a fire on the beach..."

"Ah ha! There you have it. You brought fire in your ship's tinder box. Fire from outside the enchantment. Fire is the breaker of enchantment. When you did that, the spell was broken. I felt it. The next day I sent Sharlaugh to look for you."

There were tears in her eyes, and she was breathless for joy. Robert, for his part, recalled the noise, a noise like thunder, they had heard that night on the beach. It had been, he now surmised, the sound of the enchantment breaking.

"Take me with you! Take me off this island forever."

"Una, no!" Sharlaugh almost jumped out of his seat, as if he would grab Una by her arm and hold her against her will. The other elders whispered among themselves, their gestures if not their voices indicating some controversy among them. Finally they seemed to reach a consensus. They turned as one to deliver their verdict, each speaking in turn like a chorus.

"There is so little we know for sure about this spell."

"We are not Druids, you know."

"Alas, all the Druids were killed along with your father."

"But, think of it. We have all been in enchantment for more than a thousand years. You can't just break an enchantment as if it were an empty glass. The glass is full, and all of us, including you, Lady Una, are in it. If we returned with these stranger to their land and time who knows what would become of us. For all of us the accumulation of years would fall all at once upon our shoulders. Why, in a second, in the twinkling of an eye, we would all grow old and turn to dust."

Robert remembered the story of Oisin. But Una scoffed at the old men.

"You make excuses for corpses. For me, I am not afraid to die if that is what it means to be free. Come. It is time that I claimed my dowry."

"Your dowry, my love?"

"Did I not tell you MacFinn left the Stone of Lir here, on the island. It is the anchor for his spell, without which the spell would float away. And it suddenly occurs to me, as if I have dreamed it all but forgotten, and suddenly now I remember, I know where it is. Come."

9

The day was old, but not yet spent. A cold westerly wind had brought in a dark, heavy sky, which made it seem later in the day than it was. Now the air was still, and the low, rolling clouds were yielding a fine misty rain that caressed Una's face and settled like a fine dew over the brown felt cloak she had pulled over her shoulders.

Her heart was a turmoil. It was painful to remember those events so long ago. But it was one thing to tell the tale, another to walk right into it. You could tell the tale, and still stand outside it, outside the hurt, outside the despair and hopelessness.

She hadn't even managed that. Now as they walked towards the barrow she felt she was stepping right into the past. She wasn't just recalling it, wasn't just narrating events difficult to remember but distant; she was confronting it as a physical reality—the barrow. It was supposed to have been her father's burial place, until the sea pre-empted it.

And the worst thing was, this made her hope. Hope that the past contained the seeds of the future, that in the barrow was the possibility of liberation, that in reality there was freedom from illusions. And hope bred fear. And fear, despair. Something in her wanted to deny hope, wanted to turn back, but Robert kept her going. He gave her strength. This man who was, despite the Matrix, a virtual stranger, who called himself one of the "middle nation," whose people even were unknown to her—he gave her strength. Yet she was not sure she wanted to be strong. It would be easier to admit her weakness.

She stood now at the base of a path that led directly into

the past, directly to the center of the enchantment itself, to the place that held the key to all that had happened. The events of the last twenty-four hours made her head spin. The first real events in more than a thousand years! It was exhilarating. But these events were nothing compared to the adventure on which they were about to embark, and she could not be sure, now she stood at the threshold, if she had the courage to follow this course to the end.

With all these thoughts in mind she led the way along a familiar, but now mostly overgrown trail, carrying an unlit torch. Robert brought the tinderbox from the ship to light the torch with when they got to the barrow.

As she picked her way, sometimes uncertainly over the often wild terrain, she explained to Robert why MacFinn had left the stone in the barrow. The barrow was considered a holy spot, a place of power. A place of power amplifies whatever magic mere men may make. A small spell becomes great if it can be made to "resonate" off the more potent forces of nature and earth.

"Still, I do not understand," Robert said. "To leave a stone of such value and power is a great sacrifice merely for the sake of vengeance."

"Malice is ofttimes more powerful than self-interest."

"That is true. I have often thought that if all men considered only their own self-interest then none would ever go to war. But then...."

"Then what?"

"Some men have different notions of self-interest. For example, the king of England ..."

"This is your king?"

"No. I told you. I am of the 'middle kingdom.' My forefathers came to Ireland with King Henry of England, the Second, not the Third. But we have since found it necessary to make alliances with the Irish and to follow their customs."

"And the king of England finds this contrary to what he considers his interest?"

"He does. So I, and some others of my race, have found

it in our interest to support the claim of a Scot to be king of Ireland."

"But you are not Scot. How is this in your interest?"

"Because if the king of England succeeds in asserting his authority over all of Ireland, he will punish those of us who have made alliances with the Irish and who have adopted Irish customs."

"Such as yourself?"

Robert nodded. "Whereas a Scottish king will not. He is Gaelic, like the Irish. Besides, he won't succeed."

"I do not understand. You are supporting a Scottish king because he will not succeed?"

Robert reflected that if O'Leary could hear him now he would be angry. O'Leary really wanted Edward Bruce to succeed.

"He will prevent the English king from succeeding, which is what 'we' want. No man will be king of the Irish. The Irish have never had a king, except in legend."

"Too much malice?"

"Or self-interest. I am not often sure which."

"It should be in everyone's self-interest to have a king. Otherwise you will have English kings and Scottish kings instead."

"Perhaps it is malice, then. There is plenty of that. Among the Irish."

Una walked ahead, deep in thought. She had a good, athletic stride, and he had to work to keep up with her. Suddenly she stopped and looked at him earnestly.

"My father tried to unite the land. He had ambitions to be king. But he needed MacFinn. And he needed me to marry MacFinn. Without the marriage, there would be no alliance, the whole plan would fall to pieces. When I refused, it was his ruin. Do you think I was wrong?"

"No. From what you tell me MacFinn was an evil man."

"But if I had married him, perhaps my father would be alive. Perhaps the land would be united, my father would be king. Would this not be in everyone's interest?"

"Not yours. Not anybody's. How could any kingdom founded on such an alliance truly prosper? It would rot from within from its own hypocrisy."

"Who knows on what foundations kingdoms rest? You yourself speak of English kings and Scottish kings and Irish kings as if they were sides of a dice you roll."

"Then you should feel no remorse. MacFinn was but one side of a dice your father rolled. You another."

They had come to a large, grassy mound. Robert gestured the others to remain well back and they proceeded together, silently now. In parts it was so overgrown with thorny brush that Una tore her dress and scratched her bare arms as she stumbled on the uneven ground. The place seemed suddenly unfamiliar, though she knew this was the spot. She became confused, turning this way and that.

Robert was standing by her side when she vanished, as if swallowed up by the earth itself.

"Una!?" he cried.

"I'm here."

Her voice seemed to come from the air itself. He followed it, uncertainly, as if groping his way in the dark, and in the process lost his footing and stumbled into a bush. The ground seemed to disappear underneath him and he fell, a scattering of pebbles and dirt cascading along behind him.

"You seem to have a way of stumbling into things," Una said, brushing the dirt from his hair and laughing. The laughter echoed hollowly within her breast. In truth her heart felt like lead.

He found himself inside the barrow, a pathetic pale shaft of light playing upon the cloud of dust that his descent had raised.

"Is this the place?"

"It is. Now light the torch. It gets dark within."

Before he could do so Una let out a muffled scream, gripping him fiercely by the arm. His eyes were still straining to adjust. Looking at the ground he thought he saw it move.

"Snakes," she growled, in a deep guttural voice. "The place is full of snakes."

He lit the torch, clumsily, and held it up. The ground writhed with a vision horrible to behold, a vision that seemed almost unreal, as if the dark and the torch were playing tricks on his eyes, etching lines across the face of substantiality. Yet the vision was real enough and at that moment a snake passed over his foot and another coiled around his ankle. With an uncontrollable shudder he kicked at them.

"In the name of Saint Patrick," he said, and at the mention of that name the snakes seemed to disperse and become fewer, making a thousand whispered sounds like the rustling of fine linen as the mirage of intertwined and coiled reptilian bodies vanished into the shadows.

The few that remained he poked with the torch and hurried them along, raising an odious smell of burning snake flesh.

Una breathed a sigh of relief and took the torch from his hand. He caught the look in her eyes as she took the torch and its light passed briefly across her face. She was shaken with horror and revulsion. This made her seem more vulnerable than she had ever seemed before. It made her beauty, which a moment ago he had held in awe, seem diminished, shallow and frail, as if at any time it would fall away and reveal nothing but plainness, even ugliness.

This woman is more than a thousand years old, he found himself thinking against his wish, recalling her naked, thinking of her flesh ancient and decayed. A thousand years old.

It was the place. The barrow put such thoughts into his mind. It was an evil place. A pagan place of power. It wasn't just his perception of Una that was affected. It was as if he had also been offered a view of his own mortality. It was a feeling that left him profoundly disturbed. His legs felt loose and ungainly, and his head felt like a balloon. He shook his head now, as if this would dispel the unwanted thoughts.

"Follow me," Una said, removing the heavy felt cloak and depositing it on the ground.

"Let me," he said, holding out his hand to take the torch back from her. She would not give it to him.

"This barrow was to have been my father's resting place. I shall go first."

"This is a grave?"

"It was meant to be."

That, he thought, explained his thoughts and feelings. The cold and damp touched not just his body, but his soul.

She led him down a tunnel. The passage was built from uncut stones that made up the walls, and huge slabs above which formed the ceiling, over which the mound was made. As they proceeded, the way grew smaller and smaller, and as it did he thought the weight of the earth over their heads in some way increased. They were compelled first to stoop and then to crawl upon their hands and knees. In front of him Una's shadow cast him into almost complete darkness and he had to hold onto the hem of her black gown so as not to lose her in the dark, just to satisfy himself she was still there. Occasionally he could hear her shudder and pause and knew she had encountered more snakes. But these did not stop her. He heard the torch sputter and heard the whisper of their scaly skin against the cold stone as they fled the fire, and occasionally he smelt their burning flesh as she made contact with the torch.

Finally they came to the central chamber where they emerged from the tunnel and once again could stand upright. The dank, musty odor here was more pronounced even than in the tunnel, but there were few if any snakes. Una placed the torch into a handle in the wall.

The cavern was large, at least sixteen feet across and just as high. The light of the torch seemed to be swallowed up in the dank, cold peripheries of its roughly hewn wall, but as his eyes adjusted he could make out various treasures piled around the room: gold coins, necklaces, headdresses, bracelets, strings of pearls, a coronet of abalone—all part of Una's dowry. Suddenly Robert felt very small and inadequate, for Una was obviously the daughter of a great chieftain. He, on the other hand, was completely unworthy.

Then as he stared a faint bluish light focused upon the retina of his eye, almost unreal and insubstantial at first, but gradually materializing.

"Do you see it?" he asked.

"No. Perhaps I am not meant to."

"There. It glows!"

He took a step towards it. Una placed her hand upon his arm, holding him back. In her eyes he sensed doubt and uncertainty, even foreboding.

"What is it?"

"I am frightened."

Coming from a woman who had just led the way through a pit of snakes the statement puzzled him.

"Why should you fear?"

He closed the distance between himself and the faint bluish light in three strides, then, glancing quickly back to Una, who stood frozen in her spot, he reached out with his hand until he had blotted out the radiance that emanated from the stone, then closed his grip upon it firmly and resolutely.

Something hard and substantial met his senses. Within his hand it seemed to move as if alive, like a bird or some small creature struggling against him. He almost dropped it in surprise. Slowly he opened his fingers just enough to see a small part of it, afraid to open his hands completely for fear of dropping it, for fear it might leap out of his hand on its own volition.

As he gripped the stone his hand tingled and burned. A sensation of numbness spread up his arm, followed by a ringing in his ears and dizziness. As the world began to whirl, spinning around him with multiple visions and images that ascended upwards in front of his eyes as if he were falling into an infinite abyss, sparks seemed to fly out of his hand as it grasped the stone. It felt as if the whole universe were shattering, not just himself, but the entire fabric of the world.

Only gradually did things return to normal. For the first

time he saw it clearly—not a blurry haze of bluish light, but a perfect gem, radiant with its own light, without a flaw, shining with magic. A feeling of joy overwhelmed him. Not just joy, but power too. Power and a feeling that any potentiality he could dream of was there within his hand. It was the complete opposite of the profound vulnerability and unworthiness he had only moments before experienced. As he held it, the muscles in his forearm and wrist tensed, and he laughed, turning and holding it out for Una to see.

"Throw it into the sea," she said with a sudden harshness. "It frightens me."

He hardly seemed to hear her. Fixated on the gem, he marveled at its beautiful color, and marveled too how it seemed to vibrate in his hand, sending through his arm a peculiar sensation. It was not an unpleasant sensation. In fact, it seemed to impart energy to him. It gave him a feeling of strength, of well-being, of power. He felt as if nothing could harm him, as if anything he attempted would be accomplished.

"Throw it into the sea," Una repeated. "It's the only way to break the enchantment."

She reached for it, as if to take it from him, to throw it in the sea herself. Instinctively he snatched it away.

"You must be mad. A gem like this is worth a king's ransom. To throw it into the sea—that's crazy. I'm not such a fool as MacFinn."

"You don't understand. I have remembered something. I said the stone was known as 'the Stone of Lir.' I thought it was because of its color, because Lir is the god of the sea. But now I see it was meant literally. It really is Lir's stone and we must return it to him. Only that can truly break the enchantment."

Robert stared at her dumbfounded, gripping the gem in his hand ever more tightly.

"This is pagan nonsense you speak. It is pure fantasy. Lighting the fire on the beach broke the enchantment. I heard it myself. A sound like thunder. It is broken, my lady, and you are free."

"It isn't your decision. The stone is not your stone. It's my dowry. Give it to me. I don't care if I turn into dust as Sharlaugh says. I am not afraid to die. But I am afraid of this stone, and that it still has the power to enchant me. Now give it to me, it is mine. It is my dowry."

She held out her hand, her eyes blazing.

"Your dowry, my Lady? To your marriage to MacFinn? To your marriage to what—this island? Lady, trust me. I am your husband now."

But she remained adamant: "I will not live one false minute more."

"Don't speak like that, unless you call me false as well. The hours we spent last night were not false to me. Can you look me in the eye and tell me they were so to you? Can you call them false?"

His words seemed to catch her by surprise.

"I did not mean that. But surely you can see…"

He did not allow her to finish.

"I see only one thing. I love you, and I will not let you take such a risk."

"Do you mean that? Do you love me so?"

She searched his face, her intense blue eyes darting over his every feature.

"How can you doubt it, my Lady? Have I hidden it from you?"

"Very well, take the stone. I give it to you, and all this treasure too. Only take me with you. For truly you are as a husband to me, and I love you as a wife too, and never will the word 'false' again pass my lips. 'False' to me no longer exists, but only 'love,' and there is nothing false love cannot make true."

10

"You should have thrown the stone into the sea as she asked."

The Abbot's tone is harsh. Sir Robert almost flinches, but he says nothing. He is exhausted. While recounting how he and Una had entered the barrow to recover the jewel he had felt as if he were actually reliving it. He felt the cold dank air of the barrow against his skin, smelt the odor of burning snake flesh, and heard Una's voice inside his head, begging him to throw the stone into the sea. Heard her professions of love. Heard the hypocritical words "true" and "false" on his own lips.

"You were already calculating the value of such a gem, no doubt," the Abbot says speculatively. "A king's ransom, I'd wager, as you yourself assessed it. Is this why you would not do as she asked?"

"No. No. I admit, the stone had an unnerving effect on me. Once I possessed it, I wanted to keep it. But I truly had Una's interest in mind."

"Her 'interest'?" The Abbot finds Sir Robert's use of this word amusing. Sir Robert does not see the irony.

"I couldn't let her take such a risk."

The Abbot makes a face. "Of turning to dust? And yet you would risk bringing her back here to Ireland. A greater risk, if the ancient lore about these things be true."

Sir Robert does not reply. The Abbot, with a heavy sigh, rises from his desk to stretch his legs, walking around the room now as he speaks.

"Supposing for now your conjecture is true—about throwing the stone into the sea, about her turning to dust. She was not afraid to take the risk."

He pauses, deep in thought, stroking his dry, thin lips.

"*Death happens to us all,*" he says in a casual, unsympathetic tone. "*It is God's path to immortality.*"

Sir Robert says nothing, surprised by the callous remark. The Abbot sees the need to explain.

"*It was an evil thing, and an evil spell, a spell which entrapped her soul. To leave a soul entrapped like that and not to set it free is a sin.*"

"*It was not my intent to leave her trapped. I intended to save her.*"

"*How?*"

"*Why, by bringing her back here—to be baptized, of course. She agreed. She told me she would become a Christian.*"

"*So you believed you could bring her back?*"

"*Yes.*"

"*Defying time and death itself.*"

"*I had to believe it.*"

"*And it did not occur to you that in doing so you were in some way yourself a party to this sorcery, this...necromancy?*"

"*Necromancy?*"

"*Can you not see that she was already dead, that what remained of her was but a shadow? A ghost?*"

Sir Robert shudders at this suggestion, though recalling the thoughts that had plagued his mind in the barrow, he has to admit it has occurred to him before. And Father Daniel had made similar suggestions, albeit not going so far as to use the word "necromancy."

"*To love anything is to love death. We are all going to die. We are all bags of bones masquerading as life, and the flesh is but illusion. Or so I've been told, Father. If it is so, then enchantment differs little from life in that.*"

11

As he and Una watched the island fade into the haze that hung upon the horizon, Robert, feeling a foolish need to fill the silence between them with words, said, "Well, you'll be no more a prisoner of that evil place."

He let his voice trail off, sensing he had spoken carelessly. The words seemed to hover in the air in front of them, gradually mingling in the waves, gurgling in the wake of the *Black Sligo*. The sea itself spoke what he had left unsaid. The sea knew secrets he only guessed.

Una said nothing. Standing close to her Robert could feel the tension coiled inside her as she gripped the gunwale, kneading it with her palm.

Their departure had been made difficult by Sharlaugh, who had tried to exercise his authority as Una's guardian to prevent her departure. He was almost hysterical, and there is no more pathetic sight than an hysterical old man. He repeated his theory that she would turn to dust if she left the island. And if she survived that curse, what then? he asked. She would be returning to a strange land, a stranger, without family, among people with strange customs, people who did not even worship the same gods any more."

Robert had only just explained Christianity to Una. Sharlaugh's attempt to use this against him infuriated Robert, and he said many things in anger he should not have said. It made it especially hard for Una, who was genuinely fond of the old man. Only as the island gradually disappeared did she begin to relax. Finally, after waiting long enough to confirm that the island, having vanished over one horizon, was not popping up again over another, as it would if the enchantment were not in fact broken, she let out a long sigh.

"I'll go see how Brigit is doing," she said, and went below deck.

Brigit, her handmaiden, was the only other islander to return with Robert and his companions to Ireland. Brigit was several years younger than Una, with small breasts, narrow hips, wispy brown hair and a shy, girlish manner. Her slightly upturned nose and large nostrils lent her a sort of character without making her ugly. Except for Brigit all the others had agreed with Sharlaugh who said, "After a thousand years we would all be strangers in the outside world of the present time, and perhaps unwelcome ones. Here on the island we can live out the rest of our lives in peace—and then die." Only Brigit said, "My place is at my Lady's side."

After Una had gone below Robert took a deep breath of air and glanced up at the sails. A moderate westerly wind filled the canvas, propelling the *Black Sligo* homeward. Everything seemed to be going his way, including the wind. Below deck they had stashed the horde of gold and silver from the barrow— Una's dowry. There was enough to make them all rich, and Una had offered everyone a portion. Robert himself kept the Stone of Lir, which he kept in his pouch by his side. In addition, of course, he had Una herself. He felt himself a lucky man.

There was, of course, the matter of his wife, Maire. Neill, when he learned that Una was going to be returning with them had looked at Robert and said, "Does she know?" giving a twitch of his head and a roll of his eyes. When Robert told him, "No," he grinned and shook his fingers, whistling. "Trouble," the gesture said. "You're going to get burned."

Now Robert found Neill sitting against the mast, mending a tear in his cloak. He gave him a nudge and was greeted with a big, toothy grin. Jumping up, dropping the cloak he had been mending, Neill grabbed Robert around the neck, lifting himself up off the ground the way he used to as a boy. The sea air seemed to have intoxicated him. He was beside himself with excitement.

"Whoa!" Robert cried, staggering backwards, almost tripping over one of two pigs they had loaded with them in case they needed fresh meat along the way, supposing their journey took longer than expected.

"We're going to be rich," Neill blurted. "Filthy, stinking rich. Gold and jewels coming out our ears. Bags of them!"

The treasure from the barrow would indeed make them all rich, but it made Robert inexplicably uneasy. He told Neill to keep it down and surveyed the horizon silently. Una's island had dropped behind them with surprising quickness. For the first time they were confronted with empty horizons, something he had never before experienced. It wasn't the same as when they had been lost in the fog. Then, though they had been out of sight of land, a misty cocoon had enveloped them, hiding the horizon from them. Now there was no ignoring the vast emptiness in which they found themselves. It made Robert yet more uneasy and apprehensive.

He remembered the *geis* he had broken going to sea. In all the folklore of the Gaels those who broke a *geis* always incurred bad luck. He had always joked about the *geis* the old man placed upon him. He'd dismissed it casually when they were lost in the fog. Now, staring at the vast openness before him, he felt an odd sensation. It was not unlike the giddiness a man feels when standing upon a precipice.

Tom, however, was completely confident that, providing they maintained an eastward course, they were bound to sight land—most probably Galway, by his estimation of latitude.

Tom had no fear of empty horizons. "There be sailors who sail by hugging the coast," he said. "Not I. No, sir. You think the sea contains dangers. But it's the coast contains the worst—rocks, shoals, tidal currents. Besides, it's the sea that holds the shortest route, not the coast."

Robert said nothing, but continued to stare at the barren expanse of rolling waves. It was fine to speak of the shortest route, but how short was the route if one were lost? And despite Tom's confidence Robert could not get out of his mind the possibility that they were lost. In fact, the more he thought of it the more obsessed he became with the idea, and with the idea that his *geis* had some bearing on their present circumstances, and with everything that had happened since their leaving Ireland.

"The ocean's not a void, as men suppose," Tom continued, undeterred by Robert's silence any more than by empty horizons. "Men see only the surface. Sure, it is vast and empty. Those, like yourself, who are accustomed to living on land—what you can tramp with your feet, if you please—still look to the sea for bits of *terra firma*, as if its only purpose was to hold pieces of dirt, however sparse and barren they be."

Or enchanted, Robert added silently.

"You only have to look at it a little differently, though. The surface of the sea is only the beginning—the most infinitesimal of beginnings—and all that we see in all directions is not the sea, but merely the surface of the sea, the point where sea meets sky. Beneath us is the real sea."

Tom pulled his ear and grinned, revealing his decayed teeth. Robert said nothing. At this moment the line between sea and sky was blurry. As the sun set, it seemed to crumble into grains of orange and mauve and pink, bleeding its life into the cloud and haze. The boundary of sky and sea seemed to melt, and it seemed as if they themselves were sailing on an ill-defined boundary whose meaning was largely in the head.

When it grew dark he went below. Towards the rear Brigit and Una had partitioned off a section, using curtains they had brought with them from the manor house. Brigit, seeing Robert arrive, left without a word. She had set up her own small quarters immediately adjacent to theirs and she set about now trying to put this in order, beating her pillows and sweeping the floor.

It was dark below deck and there was only one small candle in their little room, so Robert took a moment to let his eyes become accustomed to the dim light. Una was sitting in the corner on a mattress improvised of spare canvas, leaning against the cold, damp planks of the ship's hull, her arms wrapped around her knees. He could tell by the bright luster of her eyes as they shone in the candle's glow that she had been crying.

She began to pour forth her thoughts to him, swallowing her tears and blurting them out as words.

"It seems like only yesterday," she said.

It was hard to explain: before this point in time the enchantment had somehow insulated her... the past had seemed so distant... she felt it as if through a wall of cotton. Now the years of enchantment fell from her mind like a dream and she was brought face-to-face with the events immediately before the enchantment just as if it had been yesterday.

"Yesterday he pinched my cheek, called me 'my sweet,' and said, 'You'll never have to marry a man you do not love.' And he took his men and rode off to face MacFinn, and..." She broke down and sobbed. " ...I never saw him again."

"It's all right," he said, stroking her head as if she were a child.

All those years in enchantment, she had never grieved. She had been frozen in time, grief and all. Now....

Holding her in his arms they listened to the lapping of the waves against the hull as the *Black Sligo* plowed through the sea, parting the water on either side, sliding over the countless fathoms of cold dark water, over more mysteries and secrets than ever the mind of man could conceive, depths beyond imagining, cold beyond feeling. The sound of the lapping waves seemed to encompass them, and grew louder. Una fell asleep. The candle, coming to the end of its wick, flickered and went out. Robert, unable to fall asleep himself, reached down to the pouch in which he kept the Stone of Lir and drew it out. The darkness within their makeshift quarters was almost total, and at first he could not see anything. Then he saw it, almost like a smudge of light in his hand. It throbbed faintly, growing in intensity until there was no mistaking it.

It shimmered. The lines of the crystal seemed hardly substantial, as if written over the air, an illusion rather than a material object. Yet there was no doubt it was real. It had real weight in his hand, and felt hard and solid when held firmly. And as it had before it produced in him a grand sense of power, as if no potential were beyond his grasp. It was an exhilarating feeling, and he could not refrain from indulging himself in it.

He thought of MacFinn. It still didn't make sense to him. Leaving the stone, sacrificing something of such great value merely for the sake of vengeance. Out of spite. Then he thought of Una, who had wanted to throw it into the sea, even though it could well have meant her own destruction. She would have thrown it away out of despair.

They didn't understand.

Neither of them understood.

He smiled to himself as he put it safely back in the pouch.

12

The next day they continued steadily on course, making good progress. The wind was fair. *Black Sligo*'s sails billowed, full and taunt with wind, and her bow plowed through the sea like a racing dolphin, dipping and leaping from one wave to the next. Yet, the horizon before them remained a gray void.

Robert grew more and more apprehensive and impatient. He was anxious to sight land and had counted on a quick return voyage given their excellent speed. After all, they had been lost in the fog for three days, but had only drifted. Surely they couldn't have drifted this far? Returning to Ireland should be a short trip, a mere jaunt. Why was it taking as long as it was?

Tom shrugged off his concerns. "There's no accounting for currents, sir," he said.

Tom was more concerned about the weather, complaining about the air, which, he said, felt "thick," and about his joints, which ached—a sign, he said, of a change in the weather. Sure enough, in the afternoon a dense bank of black clouds began to assemble themselves in the ship's path, slightly to the south. The clouds had a sinister greenish tint, and the sea began to "make up", the waves becoming choppy, heaving with an unseen energy from the deep. The wind became erratic, dropping suddenly, then changing. Before nightfall they noticed flashes of lightning on the horizon to the south.

That night when Una had fallen asleep Robert again fished into his pouch, feeling for the smooth, cold contour of the Stone of Lir. Removing it, he regarded it in the dark, turning it over in his hands. He felt the same curious attraction to it that he had when he first touched it in the barrow. It seemed to pulsate as if alive, and exercised a strange power over him, possessing him with a feeling of elation and expansiveness.

But it also disturbed him and made him uneasy. There was something wrong, indeed false, about such feelings. Especially if he looked at the facts objectively. Looking at the facts objectively quite the opposite was the feeling he got. Then he was forced to conclude things weren't going that well.

Just the task of getting together a small *kern* and taking it from Kerry to Donegal had not gone well for him. He'd mustered only six men so far and had counted on finding the rest when he got to Donegal. He'd chosen to go by sea instead of land, tempting fate and his own *geis*, in the hopes of making better time and avoiding danger, but instead he'd gotten lost. Now even getting to Donegal in time was not a sure thing. Even getting there at all wasn't guaranteed. Worst of all, he had fallen in love—yes, he had to admit that's what it was—with a woman who had been trapped in an enchantment for over a thousand years, who was not even a Christian, and in an act of complete stupidity he had promised to marry her when they returned to Ireland, even though he was already married.

Putting the stone back in his pouch, Robert tried to get to sleep. But the ship lurched and pitched like the thoughts in his head. He slept little that night.

By morning the *Black Sligo* was plunging wildly through a heavy sea. Robert came on deck to find Neill in considerably less boisterous a mood than when they had started, his cape wrapped around him as he cowered in a corner, his face a sickly shade of green. Many of the others tried to put on brave faces, but their complexions gave them away. Except for Tom and the other seasoned sailors only MacErin seemed indifferent to it all, and Robert tried to stick with him as much as possible. The others made him sick just to look at them.

"The worst of the storm's to the south of us," bellowed Tom. "We'll be all right providing it stays where it be."

Robert didn't like the part about "providing." Pulling some thread from his tunic he tied it to the rigging so he could keep an eye on the wind. He was no sailor, but he wanted to see things for himself, not just accept what the pilot told him, and for the rest of the day he kept a close watch on the thread on the rigging. As the wind increased the pilot ordered the sails reefed, maintaining just enough canvas to keep the ship's bearing. There were two men on the tiller and every time the *Black Sligo* crested a wave they struggled to keep her heading straight; she wanted to yaw first one way then another, something that was extremely dangerous under the circumstances. Every time it crested a wave, Robert could feel the vessel lurch; he could feel it in his stomach. He would stare over the deck into the trough of the wave, just at the point where the ship began its descent into it, and he would wonder if it would ever come out of it, or whether it would just keep on sinking and sinking, down and down to the bottom of the sea. If, indeed, there was a bottom to the sea. As the ship ascended to the crest of the wave he wondered if it would it take flight. Would it leave sea and water behind and be ripped apart by wind and storm?

Eventually the cross-action of the waves became intolerable. The motion was so violent that several water casks came loose and broke apart in the hold, seriously depleting their supply of fresh water. Seeing that they were in danger of being swamped with each wave, Tom gave the order to scud. This entailed running before the wind with only a storm sail, keeping *Black Sligo's* stern to the storm and letting the wind take them where it would.

There was nothing else they could do except pray for the forbearance of Providence, which they did, drawing lots for a pilgrimage to a shrine of the Virgin. The lot, as it happened, fell to Robert himself.

"What does this mean?" Una asked, not understanding the ritual.

"The Virgin Mary is the Mother of Our Lord, Jesus. We have prayed for her intervention to calm the seas. In return I will make a pilgrimage."

"If she is a mother, how can she be a virgin?" Una asked.

Robert tried to explain, but without much success.

"She is a goddess, then?"

"No. The Mother of God."

"Which God?

Jesus. The Son of God."

"Which God is he son of?"

"There is only one God."

"But you said this Jesus was a god."

"Not *a* god. He is God."

"You confuse me. You say Jesus is a god, and his father is a god, but then you say there is only one god."

Robert tried to explain the Trinity, but again without much success.

"Perhaps you should pray to Lir, god of the sea. I fear he is angry. Perhaps he wants his jewel. You should have thrown it into the sea as I told you to."

"Una. You must not talk like that." He reminded her that she had agreed to become a Christian.

"Of course. And so I shall. But it wouldn't hurt to pray to Lir as well."

"No!"

The anger in his voice surprised her. It was as if he had struck her. She drew back, her eyes ablaze with indignation.

"Una," he said, speaking in a softer tone. "You must forget the old gods. They are no more."

"Have they all died, then?"

"Yes. Died."

"Including Lir?"

"Including Lir."

"So much has changed. I don't know if I will ever be able to understand it all. Mothers who are virgins and gods who are their own father."

She let out a sigh, then added, "But I certainly hope you are right. Especially about Lir."

13

The worst of the storm broke overnight, sometime after Robert pronounced Lir dead. He regarded this as propitious, and said so, but was not so happy to learn that the pigs, which he had ordered brought below deck, had not been, and were now nowhere to be seen.

By morning the seas were moderate, undulating like a gray sheet of silk under a gray sky. The ship bounced somewhere in between the two grays. On every side the horizon faded into mottled masses of gray, clouds and veils of rain and spray. The absence of color was so complete even Reginald's nose, usually a vibrant red, was indistinguishable in color from the sky or the sea.

Those who could broke fast. Those who couldn't cowered close to the railing. Or grumbled.

"Where the hell are we?" Robert demanded.

"The storm has blown us north," Tom said.

"How far north?"

Tom shrugged. "Who's to say?"

"Can't you tell?"

"Not unless the sky clears. For now I'd say"—he shrugged again—"a good way, sir."

The others were no more happy with this reply than Robert. They wondered aloud if they would ever get home.

"The sea holds nothing but emptiness," they moaned.

"The sea has swallowed up better men than us."

Everyone had an opinion, and most opinions involved various assessments of bad luck. Some traced it to the fog. Others to the island. Robert, though he said nothing, traced it to his childhood and the old man and his *geis*. Others, however, suspected that either Una, the Stone of Lir, or both, were somehow involved, though they too did not say so directly, only hinting ominously of ancient curses, witches and pagan spells. As time went on this opinion gained in currency, though Robert was the last to know.

They continued in this mood the rest of the day. Then, as night descended, a incredible sight appeared in their path. In the distance was a vision which shocked their senses and struck them dumb with amazement. It seemed the ocean itself was ablaze with fire that flared from the deep and shot up into the pitchy darkness of the sky. Upon approaching closer they observed that it was not the water that burned. Rather it was an island. Great flames leapt from a peak in its center and rivers of red hot liquid poured down its slopes and entered the sea, resulting in huge columns of steam and smoke ascending heavenward.

They watched in awe throughout the night, and as morning broke they approached as close as they dared, struck with trepidation. None of them had seen anything like it before, though Tom, as usual, professed to have heard stories of such places. As they sailed closer they observed the great rivers of fire that solidified upon reaching the sea. Even as they watched the island grew in size, claiming an ever larger territory from the sea and causing the sea itself to boil and clouds of steam to mix in the acrid smoke. The latter occasionally engulfed the ship, subject to the whim of the breeze. It seared their lungs and made their heads spin and their ears ring.

"This is one of the many vents of Hell," Tom said, "and if inhabited, most certainly it is only by demons and minions of Lucifer."

"Then let us begone from here."

That proved to be not so easy. The wind by now had dropped considerably and the current was against them, making their progress painfully slow. The rest of the day the island of fire dropped unwillingly behind them, and clouds of sulfuric ash followed them, covering the deck with a thin coat like silt, irritating their eyes, and clinging to their clothes and bodies, choking their lungs and throats. Only towards evening did the air become fresh again.

That evening Robert once more slept fitfully. He felt dirty, and for the first time in his life, old. A deep despair seemed to eat away from the inside of his chest. Even Una could not comfort him. Rather, he thought, she almost symbolized his despair. Was she not a thousand years old, he heard himself ask? For the first time he himself wondered if she were a witch as the others seemed to believe. Could this be the reason they found themselves in the predicament they did?

As he had done before, he shook his head as if to clear his mind of such thoughts. Eventually sleep came.

When day broke they had come upon another island, this one entirely of ice. It was comprised of huge jagged white cliffs, so dazzling in the now bright sun that it blinded the eyes to behold. The light, reflecting in the water, made the sea a brilliant shade of azure, flecked with flashes of cold fire that flickered over the waves without quite seeming to be a part of them. This had the effect of further blinding them so that the sun, sky, sea and ice seemed to mingle in a random mosaic that was in constant flux.

As usual, Tom had a story to fit the occasion.

Judas Island," he said curtly, as if the story of Judas Island ought to be familiar to everyone. When it became apparent it was not he explained how according to legend Judas, because of some small act of kindness to a leper, was granted one hour's respite every year from the flames of Hell, that to be spent on an island such as this, there to cool himself down before returning from whence he came.

"After an hour in such a place," MacFael said, "any man'd be glad to return to Hell just so's he'd warm up a bit. Says I."

He rubbed his own hands together vigorously, for the breeze that blew off the forbidding cliffs was as brisk and cold as a knife.

All the men strained their eyes to see if they could spot the arch-sinner, but even as they watched the frozen terrain moved and in a great churning convulsion of spray and mist rolled head-over-heels, sending out a huge wave that rocked the ship. Had they sailed too close the *Black Sligo* could well have been smashed into a thousand splinters, or capsized by the surge of ice and water, and Robert recalled the Isle of Satan's Hand which Tom had described when they had been lost in the fog.

"What kind of island is this?" asked Neill.

"No island at all," replied Tom, with a wink. "Just a piece of ice floating in the sea.

As they passed the drifting white mountain, awash now with cascades of water, the crew began to wash the decks, ridding it of the previous day's ash, and Robert and the others, stripping naked, poured buckets of ice cold water over their heads. It seemed to raise their spirits. Seeing them, Una laughed, covered her eyes and went below with Brigit.

14

In the days that followed they were hampered by contrary winds from the east, against which they could make no progress. Rather than fight futilely against them Tom steered a course to the south in the hope of picking up westerly winds. It was a logical plan, but not one that was greeted with much enthusiasm. The mood of the men sank to new depths of gloomy pessimism. They talked incessantly of home, and despaired of ever reaching it. Stories began to circulate about the Western Seas, about maelstroms that swallowed up men and ships, of monsters that rose out of the deep, of interminable wastes of water unnavigatable by ships and of zones called *antipodes* in which the air was unfit to breathe and which were inhabited instead either by demons or by the dead, perhaps by both.

In the evenings Sean sang a ballad that told the story of the voyages of Maelduin, an ancient hero who undertook a voyage over the seas in pursuit of his father's murderers, intent on vengeance. Seeking advice from a wise man, he was told to select seventeen companions, no more and no less. But upon his departure his three foster brothers hid themselves aboard the boat, and this brought their number to twenty. As a result, they found themselves trapped in the enchanted seas, where they visited island after island, but could not find the men who had murdered Maelduin's father, nor, they then discovered, return from whence they came. They visited an island of beautiful maidens, who took them as husbands but then would not let them go. They were fed a food that tasted to each like their favorite food, and drank wine that intoxicated them but never left a hangover. Another island stood on a pedestal, so that they could sail under it but could not land upon it, and another was surrounded by a wall of water

During the course of their many travels they came to an island where the inhabitants all stood on the shore laughing and pointing at Maelduin and his companions. They would slap their thighs, and make jokes, hooting and hollering, but when Maelduin greeted them and asked them what island this was, or what they found so funny, they ignored him completely, and continued to laugh and joke among themselves. Finally, Maelduin sent one of his foster brothers ashore to find out what he could, but as soon as the foster brother touched land he turned and joined the inhabitants, laughing as they did, slapping his thighs as they did, and hooting and hollering as they did, and nothing Maelduin could do or say could prevail upon him to return, so they sailed on and left him there.

Subsequently, they came to another island inhabited by people whose skin was as black as jet, and who were dressed also in black, and they were all lamenting, wailing and crying with grief, and they too ignored Maelduin and his companions' salutations, and continued their lamentations. Again, Maelduin sent one of his foster brothers ashore to find out what he could, but again the brother only joined the lamenters, wailing and crying in grief, and nothing Maelduin did or said could prevail upon him to return, so they sailed on and left him there.

They came to another island on which there was a castle full of treasure, brooches and ornaments of gold and silver and precious gems. There was no one there, but a banquet had been laid out as if for them, and they ate and drank. The third foster brother, whose greed was aroused by the treasure, and by one beautiful golden torque in particular, proposed that they abscond with it. He ignored Maelduin, who warned him not to touch any of the treasure, since doing so would violate the hospitality of their host. "What host?" the third brother demanded, and he grasped the necklace greedily. Instantly, he burned up and turned to ashes.

With all three foster brothers now dead, Maelduin was finally able to return home, but he was a different man and it was said he was incapable both of joy or laughter, or of grief or sorrow, and was, as well, indifferent to wealth or riches, living the simple life of an ascetic. And, it goes without saying, no further thought or desire of vengeance ever crossed his mind.

As Una listened to this tale she grew more and more uneasy. Though she said nothing, she could not help but wonder if she were not like Maelduin's foster brothers—an unwanted guest who brings bad luck and act as a jinx.

Robert, for his part, began to be perplexed by a quite different concern. He still could not shake from his mind those fragments of memories of another life, a life he had shared with Una. Often he would lie awake while Una slept and run them through his mind, savoring them as if they were sweets. He became completely convinced that these "memories," which Una had said were not real, were in fact real, perhaps more real than his recollection of Kerry, of Maire, O'Leary, or anything else in his "other" life. The intensity of these "memories" was matched only by his inability to recall more than fragments.

Frustrated, he began to press Una for more details. In the dark hold of the ship, their small space lit only by a single candle, they whispered between themselves.

Did she have the same recollections, he asked, or were hers different?

The same, she said.

How did she know that? He'd never told her what he remembered. She'd shown no interest.

"I know the Matrix," she said. "I don't need to know the details."

"But I do. I'm not an expert in this—'Matrix.' I have only fragments of memory, like tokens. Help me make some sense of them."

She considered this. Slowly, she gave a nod. Ask away she seemed to say.

"Do you remember a waterfall?" He began with the most vivid of the fragments he could remember.

"Yes."

"Where was this waterfall? On the island?" He was puzzled

because he had viewed the entire island from the cliffs and had seen no terrain such as this.

"No."

"Where, then?"

"Before the enchantment, when the island was part of the mainland, the waterfall was part of my people's land, about a morning's ride inland."

"*Before* the enchantment!" His mind reeled as he absorbed this bit of information. "How could I recall events before the enchantment?"

"You do not. You imagine them." She was curt. Abrupt. As if he were a pestering child.

"How can I imagine truly places I have never seen?"

"I have told you before, it is the enchantment. These events are all part of the Matrix."

"But you share this memory."

"They are all part of the Matrix," she repeated.

"How can two people have the same memory unless it be true? People do not dream the same dream."

"These things are all part of the Matrix."

He bit his lip. If all she would do was repeat that, he would ignore it. He let a long silence hang between them. The silence made her uncomfortable.

"I have told you before, it is not real. It is all illusion. Like the islands. Like mirrors set against each other. Don't you see?"

"No. I do not see. Mirrors are mirrors. And this—" he held up his hand "—this is a hand. It is real."

He reached forward and touched her cheek, playing with a strand of hair.

"All I am asking is for you to tell me what you remember. What happened by the waterfall?"

"You don't remember?"

"I told you, Lady. I have only fragments. My mind is not trained in these things, as is yours. I am out of my depth."

Now it was she who let a silence hang between them. He was forced to plead.

"Now tell me, Lady. I beg you. What happened by the waterfall?"

She smiled. Though she herself only wished to forget, wished to have nothing to do with anything which had to do with the enchantment, she was touched by his need to remember. The life they had shared together might be an illusion, but they had shared it, and this bound them as they would not otherwise have been bound.

"My father's bull had strayed and an expedition had been mounted to bring him back. You and I got separated from the rest. I think we both intended it to happen, though neither of us planned it or spoke it. We found ourselves by the waterfall and I remember seeing you looking at me and I knew, I don't know how, but I just knew at that moment that you loved me and that I loved you."

Then she added in a more solemn tone: "And that's the real reason I refused to marry MacFinn."

"The 'real' reason?"

"MacFinn wasn't as ugly as I made him out to be. And though he may have been selfish and mean, he wasn't as evil as I made him out to be either."

What she was saying did not make sense and he made a note to challenge her on it, but first— "Who was I in this other life? I can't seem to..."

He rubbed his forehead. He'd sensed something on the surface of his mind, and he was trying to grasp it. This made her laugh.

"You will never remember that way."

"How then?"

"You can only remember by not thinking of it."

"How can I think of something by not thinking of it?"

"How can you fill a glass that is already full?"

"You speak in riddles."

"It is a simple riddle, but an important part of the wisdom of our wise men. When you try to think of something, your mind is full of expectations. To receive anything there must first be room to receive it, and if the mind is full of expectations, there is no room. Think of that moment by the waterfall. We'd been part of a noisy expedition. Everyone was galloping around, yelling, sounding horns. Only when we found ourselves alone by the waterfall were our minds receptive to what we each must have been thinking all the time. Without that moment, we may never have known what was in our hearts. We may never have fallen in love."

"That I cannot believe. But if my mind is full, as you say it is, then it is full of you and love for you. How could I empty it? Why should I want to?"

"Then you have only two choices. Love or memory. For if you do not empty your mind you will remember nothing, and if you do empty your mind you will diminish your love."

"But, my lady, you said you loved me."

"So I do. Why do you doubt it?"

"Because you remember all. If what you say is true and one must choose either memory or love, then you have chosen memory, and cannot love."

"The answer is simple, my love," she said, poking him in the ribs, "and you are a simpleton for not seeing it. I have a bigger mind. It is capable of holding both love and memory. I am not befuddled by such things."

"And I, alas, am befuddled. You, therefore, with your bigger mind, must help me. Tell me who I was in this—other life."

"So you want your memory, too, and not just love."

"If you would humor me a bit, yes."

"You were the son of a neighboring chieftain. When you heard my father had lost his bull you came as fast as you could run to take part in the expedition, you and a bunch of rowdies you called your friends, not so dissimilar to those you bring with you now. You knew there would be a great feast afterwards."

"You're making this up as you go."

"That's for me to know and you to find out."

"And what else happened by the waterfall? I recall only that we exchanged glances."

"That is all we did, I assure you. But it was enough."

"Not enough. Not now, not then," he gave her a playful kiss, and she made a playful retreat.

"It had to suffice—then, at least. I was the daughter of a great chief. If you wanted me, you would have to court me. And court me you did, and wasted no time. But events were faster than you. My sister chose that very day to fall off her horse and by the time you went to my father to ask for my hand my father had already promised me to MacFinn. The rest of the story you already know."

Robert reflected on this. When she had narrated her story in the great hall he had never imagined himself to have been a part of her story. But then, of course, this story and that story were two different stories. Two different realities. Both part of what she called the 'Matrix,' but one being like the warp and the other the woof of a complex weaving. He would never understand it

Then she said: "Now it is my turn to ask a question of you. We are lost, aren't we?"

"We have been blown off course. Do not worry. There is no such thing as lost as long as north is north, south south, east east, and west west. We will find our way home."

"But I do worry, and so do the others. I felt it as they listened to Sean tale. There is more to this than north, south, east and west."

"Hush. Sean sings legends and fables. Leave the sailing to the pilot. Tom knows what he's doing."

But Una was not so sure. She was not unaware of the mood of the others, or that some blamed her for their predicament. When she walked on deck their eyes followed her. They did not have to speak their minds for her to know what they were thinking: if they were cursed, she was the cause of their curse.

But she said nothing to Robert. She snuffed out the candle and held him close. He was her ship, her hope, her destiny. If she clung to him, and held to him hard, held to him like the hand of the helmsman to the tiller, they would come out of this together.

15

In the days that followed Una became more and more sullen, engrossed in her own moodiness. Days passed into night under skies that were uniformly blue. The nights they shared together, as if night were a separate reality, and the sea slipped silently underneath them, uncounted, careless, without effort on their part. In the dark they made love silently, whispering their ecstasy to the night as if the night were a confidant In this way they spent their days and nights, but the days and nights did not bring them any closer to home. They covered endless expanses of water, but continued to look only at endless horizons. They weren't exactly lost, they just couldn't get where they were going. Everyone was aware of it, but no one spoke of it.

All those days of empty horizons. Empty horizons that sucked at a person's soul. Left a person feeling empty themselves. Worse than empty. As if a person had lost the very receptacle that held whatever needed to be held. Even the love she felt for Robert seemed to have drained away. There was no place in her to hold his embrace, not even a hunger to be caressed.

Their lovemaking, which before had been so intense, came to an inexplicable, abrupt end. At night she had often turned her back on him and feigned sleep, even when sleep escaped her. Once, when Robert had placed a hand on her shoulder and wouldn't accept her feigned sleep she broke down in uncontrolled sobbing, which she could not explain to him.

In the day she would hide in the dark hold of the ship so as not to gaze on empty horizons, and if she came above for air, she kept to herself, avoiding the others. But she was on deck the day they came to the island of the birds. MacErin had improvised a fishing line and caught several redfish. With the loss of the pigs they would have to depend on the sea for fresh food. Some of the tension eased a bit. Then came the shout: "Land! Land ho!" And there to the west was a large island with imposing granite cliffs. The cliffs were studded with caves, like a block of cheese. The island seemed to be populated by thousands upon thousands of birds, huge creatures with immense wingspans. They swooped down from the cliffs and rode the air currents in ascending circles into the sky. They also took a great interest in the ship and before long there were several dozen circling in the sky above it.

MacErin, who was always ready with his bow, shot several arrows at them, more in sport than out of any serious purpose. Such was his habit—to shoot whatever moved and seemed a good target.

"Oh, don't!" cried Una, seeing what he was up to, but it was too late. An arrow grazed one of the birds on the wing and it plummeted into the sea. To their surprise the other birds immediately went to its rescue and carried it off, behaving more like comrades at arms than frightened fowl.

"Those are no birds," Una cried, angry with MacErin. "Those are men!"

Indeed, as they observed more carefully, the birds did indeed have a most human-like countenance. Their faces were entirely human, accept that they had feathers in place of hair. Their bodies, too, were essentially manlike except for their wings and the fact that their limbs ended in bird-like talons instead of feet.

Over the distant island hundreds of black silhouettes began to rise into the sky and approach the ship. Birdmen, gripping large rocks with their talons and determined to retaliate for the attack on their comrade, began bombarding the ship with rocks. Many missed their mark, falling harmlessly into the sea, raising plumes in the choppy waves. Others clattered onto the deck, ripped through the sail and rigging, and sent the men scrambling this way and that to avoid being hit themselves.

Robert pushed Una, together with Brigit, who had also

come on deck, under the forecastle where it was safe, telling her to stay there until things calmed down.

Some of the birdmen swooped down in a steep dive, thus attaining greater accuracy, and so swift were they that even MacErin, who had been known to shoot a swallow out of the air at a hundred paces, failed to hit them, even though he got off several shots at close range. Indeed, one of the birdmen, who had perched himself upon the yardarm, swooped down from behind, grabbed MacErin by the shoulder and hurled him into the sea. MacErin, who was an excellent swimmer, was soon back on deck.

Reginald, in the meantime, gathered up the rocks that the birdmen had dropped on the deck and began hurling them back, but they were too large for him to hurl far and the birdmen easily kept out of his range and continued their bombardment. They were doing serious harm to the sails and rigging. Some of the rocks they were dropping were large enough to split a plank. The situation was potentially very serious.

MacErin was the type of man who had a talent for focusing his anger. Usually he focused it on the end of an arrow. That's what he did now. Dripping wet, humiliated, he picked up his bow and placed an arrow in it. His eyes narrowed and his lips tensed into a thin, taut line as he drew the bow with an inexorable, merciless resolve and let the arrow fly.

It was probably no accident that the birdman he hit was the same that had dumped him in the drink. MacErin struck him in the wing and the birdman spun in an erratic spiral, landing upon the deck where Neill, uncertain what to do, tried to wrestle him to the deck but instead got a powerful whack of the birdman's wing across the side of his head and went wheeling against the mast, falling on his backside, stunned.

Several birdmen, seeing their comrade in danger, swooped down to rescue him. This was the opportunity Reginald had anticipated. He grabbed his broadsword and began to hack to pieces any birdman who approached within reach. Blood and feathers were flying everywhere and no one else dared get close; the broadsword had a lethal range and Reginald had a way of becoming blissfully unaware of anything else when gripped by a killing frenzy.

This put a damper on the birdmen's enthusiasm, and as they were running out of rocks in any case, they decided to break off the attack. They circled the ship several times, exchanging cries that, to Robert and his men, seemed half-birdlike, half-human, and perhaps were a form of language. Then they flew off until there was nothing left of them but a thin line of specks in the distance, and these—one after the other—disappeared into the cliffs of the island. Only two remained, hovering in the distance, keeping an eye on the *Black Sligo*, and their fallen companion.

In the meantime Neill picked himself up from the deck and together with MacFael got into a tussle with the birdman. Despite having an arrow through one wing he was otherwise unhandicapped and putting up a good fight. His good wing was, in fact, a formidable weapon, as Neill had discovered, and he wasn't above biting with his teeth, just as a bird would peck with its beak. It took MacErin and Robert joining in before he was subdued. Then Reginald got rope and tied up his wings so he couldn't strike with them, and tied one foot to the mast with a short rope.

Thereafter they ignored him. Robert ordered Tom to change course and put as much distance between themselves and the island as they could, watching the two birdmen following at a distance and wondering how far they could follow and whether they had any plan to rescue their companion. In the meantime Neill, MacErin and MacFael cleared the deck of rocks and of what was left of the birdmen Reginald had killed, dumping both alike over the side like so much garbage. The crew fixed the rigging and appraised the other damage, which fortunately was very light and superficial. Then Reginald, who had been standing to the side brooding while the others did the work, suddenly announced, "I have a plan."

He began to describe in surprising detail a scheme for laying siege to the birdman's island, which he had even in the thick of combat managed to appraise. "There's a gully to the south—cuts a path through the cliffs." He made a chopping motion with his hand. "For a party of brave lads like ourselves it would be no more than an hour's brisk hike, maybe two. From the top of the cliffs we could lower ourselves with ropes and take the caves one by one. In the caves they'd have no advantage. They couldn't fly away. We'd have them dead to rights. Dead, at least."

"And all the time you're hiking up the gully they'd be bombarding you with stones."

"Thought of that. We'd do the gully under cover of darkness. Surprise 'em in the morning. I've been through worse in a siege. Climbed a wobbly ladder with nothing over my head but the shield on my arm while the bastards on the wall hurled boulders and shit and flamin' oil on us all. Compared to that this would be a piece of cake. The attackers—myself, whoever else is game for it—go *down* a rope, see, not *up* a ladder. And our mates would be up above, on the cliff—MacErin here with his bow, MacFael with his sling. Any birdman that dared attack—*fwit*! It's beautiful. Think of it. The normal dynamics of a siege— upside down."

Reginald laughed. The others stared at him, perplexed. Reginald, seeing their hesitation, grew suddenly serious again.

"You've seen the sorts of fighters they are. You're not afraid of them, are you?"

"I've no doubt we could do it, Reginald," Robert said. "But why?"

"Why?" He leapt to his feet, in a rage, spitting and flinging his arms. "Why? What kind of a question is why? Where is the fight in you? They started it. Didn't they start it? Dropping rocks on us. Throwing MacErin here in the drink?"

They all looked at MacErin, still wet, his hair matted to his forehead. MacErin said nothing, but he made an ambiguous face that somehow reminded them all that it was he who had started it all, shooting at things that had never done any harm to him, things that flew in the sky, things that were different, that were only targets, nothing more. He wasn't apologizing for it. If he started apologizing now for shooting at things that flew in the sky he would never stop, so he wasn't about to start. But he didn't share Reginald's bloodlust and peculiar sense of honor.

"Ah, but I rather think," he said, "it'd be better for us to concern ourselves with finding a way home."

"How? By sailing around in circles?"

The others nodded and looked to Robert. He recognized that Reginald's lust for battle was in part the result of the frustration and monotony of the voyage, which had taken them to strange and fabulous islands and over vast uncharted seas, but had gotten them no nearer home. Reginald's suggestion made a certain amount of sense. If they stormed the island they could make it a base. Perhaps they could find fresh water, which, considering the water they had lost in the storm, they could use. They could stay and wait for fairer winds. For men who were not by nature or occupation seamen this idea had a certain appeal, and was worth the risk involved.

You're right, of course," said Robert. "I rather fancy it may come to that. Later maybe. Right now I have a feeling we should see what other islands there are about, get the lay of the 'land,' if you know what I mean."

Reginald nodded. Robert's proposal (getting the lay of the land) had a military ring to it, even if it were somewhat out of place in a maritime environment.

16

As Una watched the island of the birdmen disappear behind them she grew even more gloomy and pessimistic than she had been before. The island of the birdmen could mean only one thing, and the faces of the others, once they had recovered from their astonishment, told her they knew it too: they had not escaped from enchantment; only sailed more deeply into it. The creature tied to the mast clearly did not belong to their world. He was too strange and too bizarre, yet at the same time too human-like, to be anything but a creature of enchantment. And as he cowered and moaned pathetically he echoed her own mood.

As she pondered this, the sky became overcast with a nondescript, grayish haze. Hanging on all sides like a dark veil, the once again empty horizon was indefinite and unsure. Beneath it the Western Sea looked almost black, like the tar impregnated planks of their vessel, which, rocking with a monotonous, sickening motion, appeared to go nowhere. Everything seemed hopeless. As hopeless and forlorn as the pathetic creature tied to the mast. They were all, Una reflected bitterly, tied to the same mast, in their own way, and the mast was stuck in the Matrix, and the Matrix would not let any of them go.

"You cannot escape the Matrix," her mother had told her. "The Matrix is everything and there is nothing outside it. And even to move within the Matrix is more than feet can do. You cannot move within the Matrix on mere feet."

Nor with sail, she might well have added.

In the days and nights that followed, Una had plenty of

time to reflect that it was that difficulty, that problematic detail, and not the storm and the contrary winds, that was the reason they had been thwarted in their attempts to return to Ireland— "Dana's Land," as she still thought of it. She had allowed herself to be fooled by Robert's bravado, by the idea that one could just blunder through it by force of will if nothing else. She had ignored Sharlaugh, perhaps her own better judgment as well. She had let Robert keep the Stone of Lir, entrusting him, an outsider, with everything. Her dowry. Her mother's heirloom. Was that right?

What had they found so far? Islands of fire and ice. A rock inhabited by birdmen. Empty tracts of water. Robert still talked bravely, but already the others were grumbling. Even their glances told her that Robert commanded them only by a thin thread of loyalty and respect. Underneath it all they did not understand him. They didn't understand the consuming passions that drove him. And they didn't understand him and her, didn't understand their love for each other. Some said he was under the spell of an enchantress—meaning her. They whispered this, not wanting their secret thoughts to be overheard, but she heard; or at least she guessed.

Only one thing interested her. After they tied the birdman to the mast, it was as if she finally had something to counter her own sense of gloom. She focused all her attention on the wretched creature. She pitied him, and pity seemed the one thing her heart seemed capable of holding onto. Because he would not let them near him they had left the arrow in his wing. He bit off the shaft, but the stub and the arrow head itself remained. It caused him pain, and bled, marking the deck around the mast with dark splotches. After they had left the bird island behind, after the two birdmen had given up the chase, after the island had sunk below and emptied the horizons again, Una told Brigit to bring her box of medicines and balms, and sat as near to him as he would allow. She had Brigit get a bowl of boiled water, into which she poured some herbal extracts, one for pain and one to promote healing and fight infection. She set that in front of him, pushing it with a pole to get it close to him. Then she waited as night settled over the world.

Now and then she whispered to him in a soothing voice, edging closer when he would allow, withdrawing slightly when he grew upset. Eventually, he drank some of the herbal tea, and grew drowsy. Sometime during the night he allowed her to touch him, and she applied a balm to his wound, then, deftly and with a skill her mother had taught her when she was a child and together they had tended wounded warriors, she pulled the arrow from his wing. He hardly flinched.

MacErin, who watched the entire procedure from nearby, commented, "I wonder would you do the same for me?"

"For any poor creature. The gift of healing is not something anyone who has it is free to withhold."

Sean, who had also been watching the operation, added, "Like the gift of song."

He leaned against the railing and sang a soft, lyrical ballad, without his harp. It was surprising how little he really needed his harp, how his voice alone could carry the tune.

"'Tis a nice song," Una said. "I think he likes it too. It helps, and you are right to compare it to the art of healing, for the soul too needs to be healed, not just the body."

Both Sean and MacErin began, for the first time, to talk freely with her as she dressed the birdman's wound. For the first time, too, Una felt comfortable with them, so she was completely unprepared when MacErin nonchalantly mentioned Robert's wife Maire.

"His wife?" she echoed.

"Aye. Don't you be telling me you did not know?" The surprise in his voice seemed false, as if it were meant to mock her.

"Why, of course," she stuttered, unwilling to appear the dupe to the deception of others. "I just... didn't know her name."

"It's a pity, really."

"What's a pity?"

"His being married. It'll not make things easy for you. A woman such as yourself, in a strange land, without a husband..."

Tears were welling in her eyes. She fought them back. She had the uneasy feeling MacErin was leering at her. Was he suggesting that he himself could take Robert's place — the place of a husband? Only a moment before she had been fool enough to think these men were showing her kindness and that she could trust them.

"Things have never been easy for me, or I would not be here."

Inwardly she fumed with anger and a sense of betrayal.

17

Una spent the night with the birdman. He had a fever and she would not leave him—partly because of the fever, and partly because she did not know what to say to Robert about her newly-acquired knowledge. She needed time to think. Think about falsehood and deception. Truth and love. Enchantments. Empty horizons.

She'd thought of the enchantment as the ultimate falsehood and deception. She'd been willing to die if necessary to end it. "Not one false minute more," she'd said. She'd let Robert persuade her against throwing the Stone of Lir into the sea. He'd spoken of truth and love.

Yet it was all false.

In the morning Robert found Una and the birdman sitting together. The birdman's head rested in her lap.

"His name is Umalekie," she whispered.

"His name?" Robert said, rather loudly, angry for having spent the night alone. He thought at first that Una had given the name to the birdman, and this further irritated him. Like naming a farm animal you might later have to kill and eat. Why should one name an enemy?

She guessed what was going through his mind. "It is not I who named him so. It is the name his people call him by."

Just then Umalekie awoke. Seeing Robert he gave a start, jumped to his taloned feet and scuttled to the other side of the mast, dragging his rope with him. Una made a calming gesture to assure him he would not be harmed. Then she took Robert by the arm, leading him several paces away.

"He is a man, only under an enchantment. And a curse. You

see, he and all his companions were given the gift of flight, and yet condemned to live upon a rock in the ocean."

Robert glanced at the wretched creature, still cowering behind the mast and regarding Robert with a mixture of suspicion and fear. He found it hard to think of it as a man.

"How do you know all this?"

"He told me."

"Told you?"

"He speaks Gaelic—a strange dialect I've never heard before, but nevertheless quite understandable."

"Those I heard spoke only in bird cries and half-human squawks."

"No doubt they thought the same of you. A man in battle is not known for eloquence or articulation."

Her testiness took him by surprise. She seemed to have developed an almost motherly sentiment towards their prisoner. Robert thought it best not to challenge her on this. It might, in fact, work to their advantage.

"What else has he told you?"

"He tells me that on a good day, when the heat of the sun beating on the rocks of their island creates an updraft, they may soar to great heights, and they can see islands to the west."

Robert rose an eyebrow in an instinctive and unconscious reaction

"But they have not the strength to fly so far. Beyond their island there are no updrafts. They can see the islands to the west, but not fly to them. Their bodies are too heavy, their wings too short. So they are condemned for eternity to their island."

Robert said nothing, holding his tongue and his skepticism.

"They live on fish and oysters, and make their home in the caves. The caves are overcrowded, so there is a perpetual fighting over territory. The territory is not worth fighting for. It's covered in excrement, and cold and damp. But outside the caves there's no place else to live. The island is barren, and the wind howls over it all year long. The caves are their only shelter."

"To have the gift of flight, and yet be so limited. That is a cruel spell."

She nodded agreement, then added: "Yet, no different from ourselves."

"What do you mean?"

"Has it not occurred to you that we are prisoners as much as he?"

Her sharpness took him aback. Her eyes pierced his. She was speaking of them, of their love, not just the voyage. He sensed it. Still he repeated:

"What do you mean?"

"Can it be we have not reached Ireland because we were not meant to? Can it be we too have the gift of flight yet are limited—by falsehood?"

Robert became very uncomfortable. "What do you mean?" he repeated for the third time.

"I mean I know about your wife. I won't tell you how I found out. Just tell me if it's true—and do not deceive me again."

Robert was completely taken aback. There was nothing he could say.

"So it's true," she said for him.

Still he said nothing. His silence only spurred her anger. "Why did you lie to me? Why? I trusted you with everything. The Stone of Lir, my life, everything."

He could think of nothing to say. The others in the expedition mocked him behind his back. He knew it was so. They said he was bewitched. Perhaps it was true. In Una's presence he simply forgot himself—forgot his own past, his life until that point, his obligations for the future, everything. Was he, in another life, married? He knew it was so, but even now, confronted with the fact, it did not truly seem real. But he was not a man of words and had no defenses against her accusations.

"I'm sorry." He rose a hand as if fending off blows. "The night we met, the night of the banquet, the night we first made love, I was...confused. I remembered nothing of my life. I ..."

"Yes, that was the enchantment. It does that. We spoke of that many times. But you did not tell me after. In the barrow at least you could have told the truth. In the barrow you spoke of truth and love. But it was a lie."

"Not about love. I did not lie about that. I was in love. I could not do anything to risk losing you."

"What did you propose to do with me had you succeeded?"

"I don't know. It didn't matter. I would have thought of something."

"It did matter. It always matters. You should have told me."

Robert could not argue with her. "You are right. Forgive me."

"All right. I forgive you. Now give me the gem."

This time Robert seemed genuinely disturbed. "What?"

"The Stone of Lir. It is part of my dowry. You cannot marry me. You have no right to keep it. Give it back."

Robert was dumfounded. "Why, in my heart, we are as man and wife. Do you not feel the same—in your heart?"

"My heart is my heart's business. Hearts do not lie and deceive. And a dowry has nothing to do with hearts. It is just an object of value. Part of a marriage contract. And it's mine, not yours."

Her eyes flashed and her red lips were as taunt as MacErin's bowstring just before he discharged an arrow. There was no question she meant every word she said.

What do you want it for?"

"To do with as I please."

"In the barrow you said you wanted to throw it into the sea..."

"So what if I did? It's mine to do with as I please."

"I can't let you do that."

"It is not for you to decide."

Robert was devastated. He had known that he would have to face this situation sometime, but he had hoped to do so in his own time. This wasn't at all how he had planned it. Now the blood drained from his face. He drew away from her, his hand clutching the purse by his side.

"I can't let you..." he repeated.

"Give it to me," she insisted, and advanced, reaching for the pouch and the gem inside. He pushed her away, forcefully, and more violently than he intended, causing her to stumble and fall. She hit her head against a railing, and let out a cry of pain. She stifled a sob, refusing to appear weak. Robert, immediately regretting what he had done, moved to comfort her, but she turned from him and cursed him, getting up and going below deck.

Robert suddenly felt all eyes upon him, especially those of Umalekie. MacErin, when Robert looked at him, looked quickly away. *So it was you who told her*, Robert thought. Only Neill came cautiously up to him and said, "It was bound to happen."

18

In the days that followed, during which they made no landfall,
Umalekie made a speedy recovery from his wounds, thanks
to Una's constant attentions. She fussed over as she would a
child, bringing him food, changing his bandages, and keeping
him company. In the hours she spent with him Una learned
Umalekie's dialect, and he hers, so that soon they could chat
back and forth without any of the hesitant gesturing and
stuttered half-comprehension that characterized their first
exchanges.

"Where are the islands of which he spoke?" Robert asked
Una, finally breaking the silence between them.

It was not Una that answered him, but the birdman
himself.

"You's like a blind man, feeling your way with your hands,"
he said—smugly, Robert thought. "Maybe we's could be your
eyes. Maybe if you lets us. From the sky we's could see things
hidden to you, things over the horizon. Maybe islands."

"Is this a bargain you propose? That I let you free to fly
away—and escape?"

"We's got wings. Fly to great heights. But not suited for
distance. So what, though? What consequence is for you?. If
we's escape, at least we's show you the way. Or where would we's
go but to the nearest land? All you's need to do is follow. And if
there is no land, what choice we's got but to return to the ship
and be your prisoner—if thats is so important to you. What use
we's to you tied to your mast? What you do with us otherwise?
Or are you cannibals too, besides being murderers? You want to
eats me?"

Robert scratched his beard. The birdman had a point. Yet Robert had been trained by a lifetime of strife never to give up an advantage against an opponent—and right now the only advantage he had seemed to be having a rope around Umalekie's birdlike leg.

"I will consider this on the morrow. It is too late in the day now for reconnoitering."

That evening they all gathered around the brazier. Sean brought out his harp and sang a few ballads while they indulged themselves in more than the customary ration of wine. Even Umalekie was finally coaxed to join them after Sean lengthened his rope. He kept near Una, cowered whenever Reginald drew close (he remembered Reginald's broadsword more than MacErin's bow), and accepted a stale biscuit (about all they had left to eat now) which he held, they noted, with two finger-like appendages on the mid-joint of his wing. Sean also offered him a cup of wine, which he at first disdained but gradually came to enjoy once he discovered its effect. Being, as it happened, the first wine he had tasted, it's effect was to set him quite at ease.

"Tell us about your people," Sean asked at last. Sean was, of all those present, the one most interested in the less conventional things that had happened to them since leaving Ireland. "Never before have I seen... men... like yourself."

"Never see you again. We's the only representatives of our race upon this earth."

"But where did you come from? How did you come to live upon that desolate rock?"

"Why says you 'desolate'?—the fishing's good."

Sean laughed. Umalekie shot him a quick glance, as if to take offense, then laughed himself. The creature had a sense of humor.

"But seriously," Robert pressed. "Tell us what enchantment made you such."

Umalekie's dark bird-like eyes darted from one to another of his audience. A smile came to his face and his sharp, blackish tongue ran quickly over his lips, anticipating the telling of a good story. But first, he held the cup of wine to his mouth and took a good long sip.

"My people—" he said, wiping his lips and slurring his words, "—we's all descendants of the Great Egg."

"The *Great Egg*?" Robert repeated. There was a slight mocking tone in his voice which Umalekie, if he heard it, ignored.

"Long ago a fisherman, fishing he was for many days without catching any fish, drawed in his net and finded a great and magical egg. Not knowing what it was, or what to do with it, he taked it home and showed it to all his neighbors. None of them see'd anything like it either. Soon enough it became the talk of the town. They's not got much to talk about, I guess.

"So then the fisherman's wife, who's childless and past the age of conceiving, decided that the best thing to do with the egg was to try and incubate it. So during the night she slept with it, keeping it warm with the heat of her warm body, and during the day, when she had housework to do, she kept it warm by the hearth. So in time it hatched, a beautiful boy-bird the likes of which she had never ever seen, and before which she now stood in wonderment and amazement. Being childless she raised it just likes it was her own son. This was a thing her husband indulged her, 'cuz he too yearnsed for a son, someone to help him fishin' when he getted older, or just to be nice to him in his old age.

"The hatchling growed and growed and as he growed he growed more and more bird-like and began, to the consternations of the fisherman's wife, to show a liking for high places. He climbed up on the roof of their shack, and over their neighbor's roofses, and he walked along the precipices and cliffs behind the village. So one day, as the fisherman's wife watched with horror all over her face, he plunged from the top of the cliff behind the village. She thought for sure he would be killed, dashed upon the rocks below, but he spreaded his wings at the last minute and goed swooping over the village like a giant Condor, letting out triumphant howls of delight like he was a real big shot.

"Well, the village—it's all abuzz. And some thinked it was a marvelous thing, this flying boy. But some thinked it were just unnatural, maybe even perverted or something, and they called the boy-bird 'freak' and they's especially upsetted that the fisherman's wife seemsed so proud of her freak. No, and it don't help that her husband goed around boasting about his 'son.' He's so wonderful and such a help fishing. Oh, he can spots fish from the air and show his Dad where to drops his nets. And the old man, he started to outdo his neighbors, bringing home more fish than any of them and boasting of it openly. So's they getted jealous. And we all knows what comesa that.

"Things gotted worse when the daughter of a neighboring widow fell in love with the boy-bird. They did—you know, what they do—and so's she gotted conceived and all and in a very short period of time she delivered, guess what?—an egg. Well, so what'd you expect? He's a birdboy, not a human. Her mother, though, she's disgusted. She broked the egg and rallied the village against the birdboy. 'All your daughters will be delivering eggs,' she said, 'if you don't do something about this horny freak.' That's what she called him. Not just a 'freak.' A 'horny freak.' Likes it all right to be a freak, just don't try pokin' other people's daughters. Know what's we mean?"

Umalekie paused, sipping from his wine, surveying them slyly over the brim of his cup.

"And what happened next?" Sean said. He was so enchanted with the tale he could not abide even a brief interlude.

Umalekie leaned closer, as if sharing his story was a form of conspiracy. "The widow's daughter—she's appalled by the murder of her egg. To her it's like her child, just as if it had been born fully developed like a human instead of just an egg that you's use to make an omelet or somethin', and knowing what was afoot in the village, she warned the birdboy, and together they fled, stealing a fishing boat and sailing into the Western Seas until they came upon the island which you discovered all by yourselfedness. It was an enchanted island and it was a perfect refuge, for the fishermen from the village would never find it, not in a million years—oh no. So there they lived, and had many eggs and many hatchlings and our race has lived there ever since, having increased and multiplied to the number you saw."

Umalekie's tale left them all silent for several moments before they realized he had come to the end of his narrative. The sails flapped in the darkness over their heads, and the sea could be heard lapping against the side of the ship.

"So where did the egg come from?" asked Robert pointedly.

Umalekie looked at Robert, blinking. "I tolded you. The fisherman...."

"Yes, I understand. But before that it must have come from someplace. It didn't just float around in the sea before that, forever."

Umalekie stared at him in total bewilderment. Evidently he had never been asked the question before. His expression of puzzlement caused Una to laugh and press Robert's forearm.

"There's a fallacy in asking the origins of things," she said. "We can never know where things truly originate, because wherever they come from they must have come from somewhere else before that. But, if we are lucky, we can know where things belong, and where we belong."

"Oh, yes. You saided it right there. For we's belonging there on that island, and we's never done belonged in human society, nor among humans, pardon me for saying so."

Robert stroked his beard, reflecting on this. Where did he belong? Then, on Umalekie's request, he proceeded to tell their own story, everything from their getting lost in the fog to their sighting Umalekie's island. Umalekie listened with great interest, particularly to the part about the Stone of Lir and the enchantment. The others, growing bored, wandered off one by one until there was only Umalekie, Una, Robert, Sean and Brigit and Neill. Brigit and Neill sat close to each other, and Robert wondered if there were not something developing between them. Sean, whose appetite for stories had been wetted but not filled, prompted Umalekie for more.

"Is it true that from your island you can see islands to the west?"

Umalekie nodded. "Islands, yes. But they's too far away for us to visit. Still, we has many stories about them."

"What kind of stories?"

Umalekie's dark tongue darted over his thin lips.

"Lotsa them."

19

"There's an island of men for whom"—he looked at Una and, in deference to her lowered his voice— "the normal rules of modesty are totally inverse. They defecates in public, and copulates in public, but they eats and drinks as if these things were shameful, and they only does these things in private. Accordingly, the lavatory is a great social gathering place, but should anyone at such a social gathering become thirsty or hungry they says, 'Excuse me, but nature calls,' or something like that, and they goes off and has a bite to eat, locked in a small, windowless room, as if this were something disgusting they was doing."

Sean laughed, slapping his thigh and rolling on the deck.

"And another island, two islands, really, right next to each other, so close that the inhabitants of one island can watch the inhabitants of the other. So that's what they does. Each seems to mimic the other, so if one man's wife goes to market the other will pick up her shopping basket too and off she goes, and each thinks the other is doing it just to poke fun at the other. And the husband will say, 'That's foolish; you're just imagining it,' until the husband of his wife's counterpart can clearly be seened wagging his finger at his wife and saying, one assumes, exactly the same thing to her. And it's a frenzy of anger possesses them all, and they would dearly like to kill each other, but whenever they jumps in their boats and rows over to the other island to settle the matter once and for alls they finds they have only come back to their own island and their own wife, standing by the dock, and she says, 'Well, did you settle that?' And he says, 'You're not my wife, you're that other so-and-so's wife,' and she says, 'Oh, this is the last straw, the last insult, you better come home now and stop your nonsense.' And of course when he gets home he looks out the window and sees the same thing happening across the way. It's interminable and maddening, and need I say both islands has a high murder rate, because people's emotions are just on edge alls the time.

"And speaking of emotions, let me tell you, there's another island where men has solved the problem of emotions by keeping them in boxes. Yes, I kids you not. No one gets angry except that he says first, 'Excuse me while I goes to get my 'anger box,' and this is a signal for the other party to choose his box: his 'self-righteous box,' or his 'contrite box,' or perhaps he too will get his 'anger box' and then there'll be a real cafuffel. And there is an elaborate system, and many books writed, instructing people on which boxes to open in which circumstances, but no one is really allowed to open a box just because they 'feels' like it, because all their 'feelings' is in the boxes to begin with.

"And there's another island where men do not dream. They wakes up and they says, 'Time has passed, I must have been asleep.' And if someone asked them, 'What did you dream?' they would say, 'Are you mad? Do you imagine that when you sleeps your mind constructs other worlds for you to wander in? Do you thinks all that stuff exists up there in your head? For otherwise, how could you explain what you calls dreams? There must be a whole other person, one person asleep in his bed, another walking about in these things you call dreams. Do you imagines such a thing is possible?' But, of course, they do not say this, because none of them has ever dreamed and so no one has ever asked them what they dream, and they just assumes that the world they walks around in is the only world there is."

Nor was this the end of all the stories Umalekie could tell, or so he claimed. "For everything that can be," he said, "must be, and there is an island for alls of them. That is the rule here, and there is no such things as 'coulds have been' or 'mights have been,' but only different islands for different realities."

For now, however, his voice had grown hoarse and he was tired, as were they all. Robert wanted to ask him how he knew all he claimed to know if, as he said, he had never visited any of these islands and, indeed, had never been anywhere except his own little rock with its (supposedly) good fishing. But he feared such a comment might be out of place and might ruin the atmosphere that Umalekie's storytelling had created. Somewhere during the telling of Umalekie's stories Una had come to sit close to Robert. Now she leaned against him, resting her head on his shoulder, slipping into slumber. In just such a way Brigit had positioned herself against Neill and Robert could not help thinking to himself the boy was 'ripe for picking.' Carefully, so as not to disturb Una, Robert drew his cloak over them both, Una and he. They spent the night like that, curled up against the railing.

And he could not help wondering as he drifted off to sleep that if Umalekie was right there must be an island out there somewhere where he would not be a married man, where he would not have to return to Ireland to fight with O'Leary, and where he and Una could live as he had lived in his imagination that first night which seemed now so long ago when he had fancied himself living another life.

20

When morning came the sea was still, the wind a bare whisper, just enough to lift the mist like a veil from the water, not enough to fill the sails. The sky was clear, a pleasant change from the gloomy overcast they had become accustomed to, and the air smelled sweet, almost like ambrosia, full and rich with dew. It reminded Robert of a summer in his childhood he spent with his mother—his real mother before he went to live with his foster parents. There had been trouble in Ireland and they had gone to England where they stayed in Dorset at a manor by the sea. His mother, who was Irish, felt as if she were in exile and the English treated her terribly, but Robert was too young to feel anything except the sense of adventure of going to a far away place, and the smell of the ocean's air in the morning.

The trouble in Ireland hadn't lasted long. It merely occasioned a shifting of alliances, and accelerated the trend among many of the Norman knights who held title in Ireland, his father included, to adopt Irish ways. Deeply offended by the way the English treated him, and particularly the way they treated his Irish wife, as foreigners and inferiors, Robert's father returned to Ireland determined that if the English would not accept him as English, then he would be Irish. That, and the fact that without making alliances with local Irish chieftains his father could not have kept his holdings in Kerry, made Robert's fosterage with the O'Learys, as well as his choice of a wife, inevitable. Robert's fosterage began shortly after his return to Ireland.

All of this was on his mind as he breathed the fresh morning air and watched the *Black Sligo* glide smoothly over the water as if drawn by some force beyond wind or current. He talked quietly about it to Una, who watched him as he leaned contemplatively upon the railing. She said nothing, but she looked upon him with understanding and he thought perhaps she understood that the way he was torn by different loyalties did not make him disloyal, and that above all he had never meant to hurt her.

Around noon they passed over a stretch of water that was smooth as glass and absolutely clear, as if the sea itself had lost all substance and their vessel floated in the air, supported only by invisible mists. Looking down, Robert marveled how the surface of the water made but a slight distortion in his vision, a thin shimmer like a will o' wisp. Below, the bottom of the sea was clearly visible, though many fathoms beneath them. The rocks, the pebbles and mud, the seaweed that hung suspended as if in the air, like giant ferns or twisted trees—all seemed to be part of an eerie, forgotten landscape. And on the bottom ran tracks as straight as arrows.

MacErin said they looked like roads. As they peered more closely they became more and more convinced that this was, in fact, what they were—roads slicing through an undersea landscape.

As they progressed the sense of traveling over a vast panorama became more and more certain, until there was no mistaking it—they were in fact traveling over a boundless undersea country. There were not merely roads, but houses, villages, fields, fortresses. They watched entranced as the variegated undersea topography rolled beneath them, so unreal and yet seeming close enough they could touch it merely by dipping their hands into the water.

"I've heard of such countries," said Sean. "Once prosperous kingdoms in our world, some curse or fatal event has cast them below the waves. Their inhabitants, the legends say, continue to live undersea in the form of fish, and periodically their country emerges from the depths, and its inhabitants, for a brief time, take the form of men again."

"Look! There go some of the inhabitants now!"

MacFael pointed to some sleek brown shapes darting over the landscape, keeping pace, it seemed, with the ship.

"Salmon!"

MacErin shouted for joy. "Get me my spear—dinner's here."

"No," cried Umalekie. "We thinks Sean is right. No ordinary fish, those."

MacErin stared at him, then turned to Sean, who, somewhat embarrassed, only shrugged. For a moment MacErin seemed to hesitate, but then Reginald stepped in.

"Why it's just a fairy story. I'm getting tired of fairy stories. And tired of stale biscuits. Those fish look mighty tasty to me."

"Fairy story," MacErin repeated, and took his spear and climbed deftly over the gunwales, hanging onto the railing by one hand. With the other hand he tested the weight and balance of the spear, marking his swiftly moving targets, gauging the distance, the refraction of light in the water, and the speed of his prey with the instinct of a born predator. His entire body was as tense as a bowstring.

Once, twice, three times, he jabbed with his spear as a fish drew near enough to the surface to present a target. Finally, on the fourth try he succeeded and triumphantly held his spear aloft, brandishing a wriggling, vibrantly colored salmon of great size. With a triumphant hoot he hefted the trophy onto the deck, clambering back over the gunwale and standing over it like a hero.

Then, as they all watched in horror, the salmon, flapping its tail against the deck, MacErin's spear still embedded in its body, began to transform. MacErin, who had been poised to pick it up, let out a low guttural sound and drew back. First an arm sprung out from where a fin had been, and a hand grasped the spear as if to pull itself free. Then, the salmon continued to writhe and wiggle, growing in size and developing legs and a human head as well until, within the space of no more than a minute, a man—not a fish—lay upon the deck.

The man looked around, and seeing MacErin, fixed him

with so hateful a gaze that MacErin visibly paled. The man folded his legs beneath him, then, trembling, rose with a determination born of vengeance. Clasping the spear with both hands he pulled it from his body and held it, dripping in blood, above him, advancing upon MacErin. MacErin, weaponless, drew back in terror, never letting his eyes off the spear.

Suddenly the fishman arched back, his eyes bulged. A knife was embedded in his back, hurled, it soon became apparent, by Reginald. For a moment it seemed this too would fail to stop him. He reeled, now fixed on Reginald, who reached for his broadsword and prepared to defend himself. Then, letting out a last gasp and sputtering blood from his mouth, the man fell, writhing again on the deck as the last breath of life past through his lips.

As they watched, his dead body transformed once again back into a fish, skin turning into scales, limbs into fins, lungs into gills, all before their eyes.

Umalekie, approaching the fish cautiously, leaned over and inspected it. When he was satisfied that it was, indeed, dead, he turned to MacErin with a pointed look and said in a shrill voice, "Just a fairy story, you say? Murderer!"

MacErin said nothing, still stunned by all he had seen, but Reginald was less reticent.

"Keep your beak shut, you. I'm fed up with all this nonsense. Birds that think they're men. Fish that grow arms and legs. I tell you I've had enough! It's disgusting, is what it is. Unnatural. Demonic. Yes, by God's toenails, demonic! And you, whatever you are, bird or man, you're the devil's brood is what you are. Hatched from the devil's own egg. You keep out of my way, I tell you, or I'll give you a taste of Norman steel."

He glowered at the birdman, not taking his eyes off him as he stooped to pick up his bloodied knife. Umalekie, with a birdlike hop and skip, retreated. At the same moment Robert stepped between them on the pretext of picking up what now was clearly no more than a dead fish. This he prepared to heave over the side.

"What are you doing?" Reginald demanded.

"Well, you don't propose to eat it, do you?"

"And why not? It's a fish, isn't it?"

"I'm not so sure. Are you, after what you've seen?"

Reginald grumbled, but he couldn't look Robert in the eye and give him a straight answer. He didn't know the answer. He knew only his own feelings, knew that he was angry. He didn't really want to eat the fish. He only wanted to make a point—a fish was a fish. A man a man. And all of this, everything, indeed, that had happened since they had left Ireland, could not be real. It must be a dream. And as any dreamer, dreaming, says to himself "This is only a dream," and so awakes, Reginald felt some similar act would break this spell. Just as his knife had killed the fishman and made him turn back into a fish, this whole enchantment could be dealt a similar blow.

But how?

Reginald grunted and turned abruptly on his heels, marching angrily up to the forecastle, where Una looked watched him uneasily. Robert tossed the fish carcass into the sea. During the interval since MacErin had speared the fish the ship had passed into a patch of weeds, and the carcass landed with an odd, almost whimsical sound.

Robert gazed at the weeds in surprise. What, he wondered, had happened to the undersea world? It was as if the weeds were a curtain that some hidden power had drawn between them and the undersea world. It clogged their way and they no longer glided over a glassy surface, but bobbed uselessly in the muck.

Or had the undersea world been there at all? Could he be sure what he had just witnessed had even happened? Indeed, he had an odd sensation as if he were just snapping out of a dream. Sounds rushed upon him. He felt a ringing in his ears and a momentary loss of equilibrium, and looking around it seemed that everyone else was going about their business as if nothing had happened.

21

Robert has a theory, which he is trying to explain to the Abbot, that all God's creatures are the same; they are all sentient—perhaps sentient on different levels, but nonetheless sentient and therefore substantially the same. That would explain both the birdman and the fishman, beings who crossed the divisions between species, divisions that were perhaps more artificial than we like to think.

"Blasphemy!" says the Abbot, though without the same conviction he's mustered on previous occasions. "Men were created in the image of God. Men alone of all God's creatures have immortal souls."

"But is it not true that God is all-powerful? If it were God's will that a man become a fish, who's to say it should not be?"

"That is a foolish argument. It assumes that God is frivolous, that he would use his omnipotence to engage in capricious acts."

"Perhaps it's not capricious. Perhaps He has some reason we do not yet comprehend, some lesson for man to learn."

"Something he could learn as a fish, but not as a man?"

"Perhaps. Why not?"

"Because you are assuming that God created man imperfect, and needed to create the other species to make up for it, and that man, therefore, needs the other creatures to be complete himself."

"But man is imperfect. There's original sin."

"You don't imagine that's God's fault, do you? God created man perfect, and man sinned."

Robert has heard the argument before, but never grasped it. How can a perfect creation sin? But there is no point in arguing now. He is no match for the Abbot's theological certainty.

"Scripture," the Abbot says firmly, "tells us that God created all *the other species first, and then created man and gave man dominion over them. And only man has an immortal soul."*

"But I saw what I saw..."

"What you saw was a shapechanger, a powerful magician in allegiance with the devil, an unnatural, perverse deception and misuse of God's creation."

Things are not going to get any easier, Robert thinks. The rest of his story is stranger still.

Then, as if suddenly coming to a decision, the Abbot says: "Come with me."

He leads Sir Robert out a side door from his office to a large adjoining room which houses many books. This is the abbey's scriptorium, where books are copied and stored. Sir Robert would have expected a crowd of monks busy with various duties: Copying, binding, repairing, scrubbing the floors. But the reality is quite different. The room is deserted and indications of neglect are evident in the dust on the table tops and the dirt on the floors.

"I cannot claim to have knowledge myself," the Abbot says at last. "But I have books." A small laugh escapes his breast like a hiccough. "For some it is the same thing, but I wonder. Books are but words written down. Can we be sure they are the truth merely because they are written? And even if they be the truth, can we be sure we understand them correctly? Only God gives understanding. For that it is not knowledge you should seek, but faith."

The Abbot walks down an aisle, down the length of a great oak table on which various manuscripts are arranged. He passes his hand over certain of them as he goes, almost as if in a gesture of love and respect, or of benediction, as if they are his children. In a sense, many of them are, for he himself had personally copied them. Others he has commissioned or collected. The majority, though, are of ancient lineage, collected by his predecessors over a period of centuries.

The Abbot pauses. His hand strays downward and comes to rest gently upon a thick tome finely bond in gilded leather.

"Ah. Saint Finnen," he says, casually, picking the book up and rubbing its cover affectionately.

The Abbot recalls how long ago he visited a monastery in Munster where he found a manuscript purporting to be a facsimile of an original by Saint Finnen himself. It was not a good transcription, the Abbot surmised; the scribe appeared to have made errors while himself presuming to correct errors in the ancient syntax—always a risky business. But any copy of such a work was worth copying in turn, which was precisely what the Abbot did.

Saint Finnen, the story goes, had in the course of his travels over Ireland met a man named Tuan Mac Carell, a pagan chieftain who claimed to have enjoyed innumerable past lives and transmutations through various forms—stag, boar, eagle, fish and so on—of which he could recall every one, as well as observing in these forms all the events and history of Ireland from the most ancient times to the present.

Saint Finnen had recorded all his stories faithfully, even though, as a Christian, he could only accept much of the narrative with a grain of salt. That a man could, instead of dying, transform into a stag, then a boar, a fish, and so on, and in such way avoid death—this was something no Christian could believe. Yet neither could Saint Finnen believe the pagan chieftain to be a liar—a poet, perhaps, but not a liar—and, holding all the ancient lore of Ireland in the greatest reverence, he dutifully recorded every word. The Abbot, in his turn, copied the manuscript from the Donagal folio, doing the best he could, he thought, to restore the original syntax, and brought it back to Galway, where it formed part of the abbey's library, a valued treasure.

"And this book," Sir Robert says, breathless with excitement, *"does it describe the places we saw: the island of the birdmen, the undersea world?"*

The Abbot puts the book gently down. *"What can one make of such stories? That the soul of a man may transmigrate into animal, fish and bird. What becomes of his immortal soul? Did Christ die on the cross merely that men might become fish or birds? How can we, Christians, believe such things?"*

Sir Robert swallows. Nothing he has so far said has ingratiated him to the Abbot. What he has left to say would please him even less, but does he have anything to lose?

"I have...seen such things."

22

That night, in the dank dark of the hold, the still silence lent Robert a restless sleep. Dreams rose to his consciousness like vapors, forming and reforming in strange images. He saw the Stone of Lir hovering in front of his eyes, grasped it with his hand, and watched as it became a vortex of light drawing him into it.

Then he found himself on the *Black Sligo*'s deck. A fishman faced him only yards away, armed with a trident. In his own hand Robert held the Stone of Lir. He realized, too late, that what he needed was a sword.

"You forgot your *geis*," the fishman said, thrusting at him with his triple pronged spear. Robert dodged to the right, but lost his balance on the sloping deck, flailing with his hands to grasp the rail and keep himself from falling....

So flailing, he awoke, and found himself rolling off his bed of canvas. He fumbled in the dark for several moments, thinking he had dropped the gem. Then, realizing it had been a dream, he felt at his waist. The pouch with the stone inside was still there.

"What is it?" Una's voice was an soft whisper.

"Nothing. A dream."

"Tell me," she said.

It reminded him of the first time he had woken in her bed. He told her the dream as best he could remember it. She said nothing for some time. Then she said, "You did not tell me you had a *geis*."

"There are many things I have not told you. For lack of time or opportunity, Lady. Not from duplicity."

"Yes," she said. She said it casually, almost like a yawn, or a sigh. But for him that simple "Yes" was an absolution, an acknowledgment that she understood that underneath it all he was well-intentioned. Then again, he thought, he may have read too much into it. Perhaps it was just an indication of indifference on her part. Already she was dozing off again.

After Una had fallen back to sleep Robert lay awake and listened to the creaking of the rigging and to the sound of footsteps on the deck overhead. He thought of his *geis*, and of the fog in which they had been lost. He thought of when he had stood on the cliff with Una on the island and how she had spoken of mirrors set against each other and of endless enchantment. He had almost been able to see the islands in her eyes. He thought of the stone in the barrow, and remembered her words: "Throw it into the sea." Remembered too that she had demanded its return and he had refused. He felt suddenly for it now. It was still in his pouch at his side.

It was still in the pouch at his side and he was still...

He was still....

His *geis*. He wondered... was his *geis*...?

23

First thing in the morning Robert dressed and went on deck, sniffed at the air, which was fresh but didn't give him the same pleasure it had the day before, and surveyed the horizon, which was empty. Then he glanced up at the sails. They still hung limply and reminded him of curtains in a mausoleum. And it didn't take him long to see that they were still drifting listlessly in the weeds.

Remembering his dreams the night before he uttered a curse, then went to the water barrel and grabbed the cup. He had to stoop lower than he expected to fill his cup. This reminded him that they had been many days at sea and would soon be running short of water. He wondered if he ought not be giving some thought to rationing.

Seeing Umalekie sleeping by the mast something in him seethed. Umalekie talked as if he knew more than he did, yet he could not tell them where land was. He talked about islands upon islands, but could he tell them how to sail to just one of them? Abruptly Robert gave him an unceremonious kick. Umalekie woke with a start.

"This is no time for sleeping. I need your services."

"To do what?"

"Find me one of these islands you talk so much about." Robert finished his cup of water. "We've been at sea too long."

Taking out his knife, Robert cut the rope that bound Umalekie to the mast with one deft movement.

"We's can look, but we's can only find what's there." Umalekie sensed that Robert was expecting more than he could deliver.

"Then look, but mind you look well. You tell me you have seen these islands from your miserable rock. I don't see why you can't find them when I ask—unless you are playing games with me."

"No. We's not play games with you."

With a hop and a bound Umalekie was perched on the rails, and before any of the others knew what was happening he had flung himself over the gunwale as if to dive into the sea but instead, spreading his giant wings, he pulled away from the water just in time and soared up into the sky even as his forebear must have done long ago leaping from the precipice behind the fishing village.

It was several hours later before he finally returned, after ascending to such a height they could barely see him.

"What did you see?"

"Nothing."

"Nothing?"

"Nothing. Big, vast emptiness."

"But you said from your island..."

"From island. You's sailed a long way from island. Do not blame us for that."

Exhausted, Umalekie threw himself by the mast, as if he had accepted this as his proper place, whether tied to it or not. Robert began pacing the deck, deeply troubled.

"We are not sailing anywhere. We are only drifting."

"This is my fault," Una said. "Do not blame him."

"Your fault? How so?"

"It was because of me you will not throw the stone into the sea. That is the cause of all your problems. The reason you and your companions are stuck now in enchantment. Why you cannot find your way home."

She gritted her teeth, coming to a hard resolve: "Throw the stone into the sea. It is your only hope."

"Nonsense."

"You cannot deny it."

He tried to ignore her, walking on. He could deny it easily, say it was his *geis*. But he did not wish to discuss his *geis*.

"Throw the stone into the sea," she repeated. "Don't worry about me. I am ready, whatever happens. I've been ready for a thousand years. Throw the stone into the sea."

"No! I can't do that," he said loudly. Realizing the others might overhear, he lowered his voice, almost to a whisper. "If it means being lost in enchantment, I am ready for that too."

"Why did you lower your voice?" she demanded.

When he did not answer (perhaps again fearing to be overheard), she rose her voice herself—"It's true. You know it's true and you do not want the others to know. But they do know. The way they look at me. As if it's all my fault. As if without me you would all be back in Ireland by now, fighting your battles. That's all you care about."

Everybody on deck heard what she had said. They made no pretense to look away as if they had not. Angry now, Robert took her by the arm and led her towards the hatch, glaring at the others on the way.

"Do not speak like that in front of the others," he said when they were below deck.

"It's true," she repeated. Her voice cracked. She was weeping now.

"Calm down. You don't know what you are talking about. But if you get the others talking there's no telling what trouble will come of it."

"How can you keep them from talking? What else have they got to talk about?"

"They will do as I say. And you will calm down. We are where we are because we have encountered some unfavorable winds. This is what the pilot tells me."

"Oh. And is he the expert in enchantments now?"

"As far as I'm concerned Tom is the expert on how we got to where we are, and how we will get back." Robert's sudden confidence in the pilot surprised even him. "And since I am the leader of this expedition what I say goes. Is that understood?"

She looked at him, making an effort to calm herself. But it was evident she regarded what he was saying as little more than bluster and it did not impress her. Looking into his eyes she saw that he did not really believe it himself. Still, there was no point in arguing with him. Promising to get some rest and, as he said, calm herself down, she went to their makeshift room.

Back on deck Robert could feel the gaze of the others upon him, even though they avoided his eyes. He knew they had been at sea too long and were tired of empty horizons. They, like him, had hoped Umalekie would sight land. Better yet if they could catch a wind—any wind but preferably a westerly one that would take them back to Ireland. Otherwise, a bit of dry acreage. Some fresh water. Game. Anything to break the sense of monotony, the feeling of hopelessness that followed him everywhere as he paced the deck.

The feeling of hopelessness followed him below deck that evening. It hung in the stale air, lingered in the flickering light of the candle, gripped his guts and twisted them, squeezing his lungs so that even breathing did not satisfy him.

Una lay her head on his chest, clinging to him as he lay staring at the beams above their heads, absorbed in thoughts he could not share with her. She said nothing, but began fidgeting with the buttons on his tunic, undoing them one by one. She ran her hand over the hairs on his chest, drawing playful circles with her fingernail around his nipples and down his abdomen. She kissed him, and caressed him in ways no woman had caressed him before, rousing him to such passion that he trembled all over. She held him back, however, and would not let him fulfill his desire just yet, would not let him mount her. Instead she teased him with small, light strokes, strokes that barely touched, that made his skin tingle. She let her hair cascade over his trembling body as she straddled him herself.

In the height of her ecstasy her back arched and she let out a muffled cry, and shuddered. There were tears in her eyes as her body went limp and she sank down into his arms. Inexplicably she could not stop crying.

"Do not cry. Things will work out."

Robert's thoughts were in turmoil. What folly it seemed now to even think of returning to Ireland. Una would have no place there. He could not marry her. Nor would she have family or ties of her own. She would live a lonely, miserable existence.

He had always assumed he would think of something once he got her home. He had been so consumed with the necessity of getting back to Ireland as quickly as possible he hadn't given a lot of thought to what would take place once he did so. As it happened, getting back to Ireland had proven more difficult than anticipated. Already they were probably too late to be of any use in Ulster. He wondered if there were any point at all in still trying to make the muster there. If that were the case, would it be a better plan, for Una and himself, to find an enchanted island in these enchanted seas and live out their lives there together? He even wondered if it would be possible to retrace their steps and find Una's island again. There perhaps they could live in peace and be happy.

He almost said as much to Una as they lay there, but she had already fallen asleep. It could wait until the morning. The important thing was he had resolved in his own mind—returning to Ireland could wait, if they returned at all.

24

In the morning he woke to find himself alone. A sudden intense awareness gripped him, a realization that something was dreadfully wrong, something he should have anticipated. Feeling frantically among his discarded clothes he found the pouch in which he kept the gem. It was empty.

Grabbing what clothes he could he dashed up the ladder half naked. Even before he had made it all the way up the ladder he could see Una, the Stone of Lir in her hand, standing by the railing, searching within herself for the resolve to throw it into the sea.

"No!" he cried.

Several yards separated her from him, and there was no way he could climb the rest of the way up the ladder and reach her in time to prevent her doing what she seemed intent on doing. Neill, on the other hand, was sitting close nearby. Hearing Robert's shout he surmised the situation quickly and jumped to his feet, his long arm grasping Una's wrist and trying to take the Stone away from her.

In the course of doing so he caused Una to drop the gem. It clattered across the deck and seemed on the verge of tumbling over the side and into the sea. Twirling like a top it came to a stop only inches away from the edge. Robert scrambled up through the hatch and was on the verge of recovering the Stone when he was unexpectedly and unceremoniously knocked from behind.

It was Umalekie. Having been released from his bondage to the mast, Umalekie had taken to perching on the yardarm. He had been watching Una as she stood by the railing trying to find the resolve to throw the Stone in the sea. He didn't know what she was up to, and didn't understand all the hidden dynamics, but seeing what was happening now he swooped down from behind Robert and scooped the gem off the deck like an eagle scooping a fish from the sea, returning back to his place on the yardarm—all in one coherent, graceful move.

He examined the beautiful object now in his possession, entranced with its pulsating brilliance, then gaped at the two parties apparently disputing its ownership.

"Hey! Give that back!"

"Don't give it to him, it's mine."

Umalekie cocked his head and ruffled his feathers. Everyone by now was gathered around listening as Robert and Una disputed.

"I will defer on the question of ownership," Robert said, recognizing this was a weak argument for him. "But I fear my Lady is distraught and doesn't know what she is doing, for she would throw the gem into the sea, and this will almost certainly result in her death. Surely you do not want this?"

This got Umalekie's attention. His devotion to Una for all the kindness she had shown him was profound.

"Is this so?" he asked her.

"He says it is so."

Robert quickly explained to Umalekie his theory, embellishing it somewhat to give it more credibility so that it became less a theory than a truth established in folklore, unquestioned by the wisdom of tradition. Umalekie grew more and more disturbed and looked at Una as if pleading her to abandon her claim. Robert thought things were going well when Una suddenly turned and addressed the others.

"The Stone is evil. You all know it is evil. It is a curse on us all, holding us all, myself included, in the grip of an enchantment. But for the Stone you would all be back in Ireland. Do you not already know this? I tell you that it is only by throwing it into the sea that the spell can be broken. It is only misplaced love that prevents your leader from doing so himself. But I tell you if you are truly his friends you will do as I say. Throw the Stone into the sea."

Robert grew increasing uneasy and sensed danger, for in appealing to his companions Una was introducing another factor into the equation. Even if Robert could talk Umalekie into giving him back the gem Robert would have to answer to his companions as to why it should not be thrown into the sea if indeed, as Una said, that would end the enchantment and allow them all to go home. In fact, several of them, including Reginald and MacErin, were already grumbling quite vocally to this effect.

Umalekie hesitated.

"Do not hesitate for my sake," Una said. "I am already dead, Umalekie. I've been dead a thousand years. What you see is only a semblance kept prisoner by that accursed gem. For my sake you must do as I say. Throw the Stone into the sea."

Umalekie considered both sides carefully, strutting from one end of the yardarm to the other and back again many times, deep in thought.

Finally he addressed Una:

"We's cannot deny that this is your wish, and that you's the only one can judge what's best for you. But is you absolutely certain this is the best thing?"

"As certain as I stand here. That is my wish."

Umalekie appeared more distraught than Robert ever thought it possible for a man with the face of a bird to look, but Robert realized that he was leaning towards doing as Una said.

"Wait!" Robert remembered what he had been thinking the night before. "There is another possibility."

Umalekie paused, and waited.

"I will stay here. That is my wish."

"Here?" Umalekie repeated, not quite understanding.

"In enchantment. We can find one of those islands you say are all about. Or, we can find our way back to Una's island." Facing Una he said, "Sharlaugh would be glad to see you, Una. He was sore to let you go."

The proposal caught Una completely by surprise.

"You would do that?" she asked. Then— "No. I couldn't let you do that. To throw away your life like that. That's what you would be doing."

"What about us?" demanded Reginald.

"Take the ship. The treasure too. It's yours."

"What about the curse? We'd be trapped here. She said so herself. Our only hope is to throw the gem into the sea. That's the only way we'll ever get back to Ireland."

Robert had to think quickly. "If it is true the Stone is cursed, then I keep the Stone—and the curse. You are free."

"That's not what *she* said."

"That's right. She said our only hope was to throw the Stone into the sea."

They were all against him now, except for Neill, who was just confused. They were becoming belligerent, demanding that if Umalekie did not throw the gem into the sea that very minute they would come up and get it themselves. When Umalekie still hesitated MacFael, who had furtively loaded a sling, let fly a stone, which grazed Umalekie's head. Although not seriously wounded, he dropped the gem, which clattered to the deck. Robert ran for it, but MacErin was faster, and Reginald, who was not far behind, grabbed Robert by the arms, keeping him off MacErin.

MacErin looked at Robert, almost apologetically, then at Una, who gave a solemn nod. Then he wound up and hurled the gem as hard as he could into the air. It flew in a grand arch, tumbling and spinning, first gaining altitude, then seeming almost to hover, suspended for a brief moment, then falling, gaining speed as it plummeted towards the sea.

As the Stone of Lir hit the water they all froze. The small "plunk" with which it struck the water did not do justice to the irreversible finality of that small event and the consequences it would have.

Una turned solemnly and looked Robert in the eye: "It's for the best, my love. You must go home. It's where you belong."

Then she hid her face and when Robert moved to touch her she pulled away sharply.

"No," she cried. "You must not see me. I will not grow old before your eyes. I will not have you see me turn to dust!"

So saying she pulled her cloak over her, crumpled into a fetal position under it, and fell in a heap by the mast.

In the meanwhile strange things had begun happening where the gem had fallen. The water began to bubble, at first slowly, then more vigorously until a small hill of water was being forced up by the rush of air and the swell took hold of the ship like a giant hand, lifting it and turning it a hundred and eighty degrees so that the whole crew rushed from one side of the deck to the other to watch what was happening.

Robert was torn between Una and the events happening around them. Tearing himself away from the latter, he bent over and touched the bundle at the foot of the mast and was relieved to feel solid bone and flesh and not mere dust. He could feel her move under his hand, but she would not permit him to pull away her cloak. Several times he called her name, but she would not answer.

But he could no longer ignore what was happening around him. The ship lurched and the deck tilted under his feet, as if it had struck a reef. But it was not a reef the ship had struck; it was land—land which was rising from the sea. The violent tilting of the deck caused Una to tumble from her position by the mast, and instinctively she flung out her arms to break her fall. In that instant, though she quickly covered herself again, Robert glimpsed her face. Her face was as beautiful and youthful as ever, if somewhat distorted by terror.

"Una, look at yourself."

"No."

"You are not aging at all."

He knew she had heard, but at first she did not move. Then she held up her hand, and he could tell she was observing it from under her cloak.

"Una, what's happening? An island has surfaced from the sea. Out of nowhere. From the very point where the gem fell into the water."

Una shuffled under her cloak, shifting from a fetal position to a sitting-up position. The island was continuing to rise out of the sea, growing bigger all the time. But Una paid no attention to this. She stroked her cheek and held up her hand before her eyes, still afraid she was about to turn to dust.

"Look at me closely. Tell me truly, have I not aged just a little bit?"

She pulled the cloak cautiously away from her face, letting him gaze upon her. He looked closely, stroking her skin. It was as soft and smooth as a child's.

"Is there not, perhaps, just a little wrinkle around my eyes? My lips? A hair that's gray? A blemish or spot that wasn't there before?"

"No, not a wrinkle or spot or gray hair," he said, and kissed her eyes, her cheek, her lips. She turned her face away, still not certain, not trusting him in case he was lying yet again.

While they were occupied with this there was complete bedlam around them. Neill and others were vying for Robert's attention. The land that had risen from the sea was now a small island and growing all the time. The seaweed and mud that had originally covered it was already transforming itself by some magic into shrubs and grass. Already the bolder ones of the retinue—MacErin and Reginald—had jumped from the deck and were exploring the new land. They marveled at how quickly the ground was drying, and how the grass and plants were growing. MacErin said he could feel the grass sprouting beneath his feet.

Una, as she gradually began to accept that she was not about to turn to dust, began to tremble and shudder with excitement. She could barely bring herself to stand and see for herself what was happening, but she did, and laughed and cried for joy.

"I think I understand—" she began. Sean, who was standing on the bow, let out a shout, pointing towards a castle that had not been there only a moment before, but which now gleamed in the sun like a diamond—a black diamond, for that was its color. A fine mist rose off its walls as the sun hit it and a rainbow crowned it, seeming to beckon them to it.

25

The castle was a fine structure of smooth black basalt, the shape of a cube, each side of which was identical except for the side which contained the door. There were no windows, and the stark walls were some thirty feet high. At intervals the walls jutted out a foot or two so that it had the appearance of being ringed with vertical ribs, but there were no towers to speak of. Almost three times the height of a man, the doors were a half as high as the castle itself, and were of solid brass, etched with elaborate swirling designs similar to those found on old Celtic crosses throughout Ireland.

The whole retinue had, after some debate, left the ship (it was perched on a small hillock that was now about a hundred yards from the sea) and made their way to the castle. The debate had focused on two questions, the first being whether the island could be trusted to remain an island or whether it might just a quickly sink back into the sea, in which case they ought to remain in the ship. The second question revolved upon whether or not the castle was inhabited and whether the inhabitants could be counted on to be friendly.

On the latter point Reginald replied sarcastically that if it had been inhabited the inhabitants would all be dead, as they would have drowned long ago. The Irish were not so sure, and Robert himself could not help thinking about the fishman that MacErin had speared. In the end, however, nothing could have prevented them exploring the new island. Robert, wanting to take the initiative, if only to show he was still in command, decided he might as well lead the expedition. But he suggested that it was much too dangerous for a lady, an opinion supported wholeheartedly by Brigit, who had come on deck just in time to see the castle rising.

"Don't speak of danger to one who should be dead," Una said, and then added, definitively, "There is no danger here."

What justification there was for this statement she did not say, but her courage inspired the others, who would never allow it to be said that a woman's boldness surpassed their own, and in this spirit they came to the castle and hesitated only briefly before the entrance—then pushed against the heavy brass door.

It opened without a noise, its hinges gliding as if on air.

Inside they found the floor of the castle was covered in a mat of seaweed, which also hung in places along the walls. The walls themselves ran with water, which formed rivulets in the cracks between the huge basalt blocks and ran in thin sheets over the surface. From the roof, which was of crystal and let in the daylight, it literally rained, though somewhat unevenly so that by careful maneuvering most of the party was able to keep relatively dry as they cautiously, and in some amazement, made their way through the hall.

Even in the short time it took them to make their way from one end to the other the hall began to dry. The water almost seemed to boil, yet made no steam. The "rain" gradually ceased, the rivulets dried up, and even the seaweed at their feet became a soft carpet of reeds, and that upon the wall became woven tapestries. All this transformation occurred before their eyes, but in such a way that they hardly noticed it happening.

Stranger than that, when they reached the end of the hall and turned around again, they found that a long oak table had appeared which had not been there before, and at the end of it sat a pale, dark haired man of regal bearing, dressed in a blue-green robe covered with inlaid abalone that flashed in the pale light. Even as they gawked at him, the table, which they all would have sworn to be empty a moment before, was now covered with food and drink. The feast was entirely of the sea: baked fish on platters of giant clam shells, prawns laid out in a bed of kelp, scallops and mussels in a stew of oysters, and much more, all very inviting and prepared with great culinary skill and attention to appearance.

"Gentlemen. I beg you be seated. You are my guests."

The others were somewhat suspicious, but they had had little substantial to eat and were hungry. In addition, the fare on the table was tempting. Brigit, being the hungriest, was the first to sample, smacking her lips and licking her fingers. The others quickly followed. Only Robert still held back. He was transfixed by something that dangled from around their host's neck. It was the Stone of Lir.

"Where did you get that?" he demanded, trying not to sound too aggressive.

The man ignored Robert and turned to Una. "How like your mother you look."

Una seemed completely transfixed, as if nailed to the floor.

"Do I?"

Robert took another step towards the mysterious stranger.

"Wait a minute. You two know each other?"

Una grasped his forearm. "Not exactly," she said, though still transfixed by the stranger.

"Ah, dear girl. I have so much to tell you."

"You do indeed, my friend." Robert still eyed the stone. "I am Robert FitzWalter. These men are my companions-in-arms. We were bound for Ulster when we lost our way in a fog, and... but it is a long story, and I do not have the pleasure of knowing who you are, or what is this land which has appeared out of nowhere, or"—Robert grew bolder— "how you came to possess that stone which only a short time ago..." Robert hesitated to tell the whole story... "only a short time ago I had in my own possession."

"That too is a long story." The mysterious man shot a glance at Una. "*My* lady, is it? His *possession?*"

Una nodded, and the mysterious man turned back to Robert.

"I promise you all your questions will be answered"—he

sounded a lot like Sharlaugh now, thought Robert— "But first, you are my guests. I offer you my hospitality. There's time for your questions later."

He gestured for Robert to be seated. Robert removed his sword and deposited it against the wall. It would be rude to accept hospitality while fully armed. The others followed Robert's example, and their host clapped his hands and servants appeared from behind some curtains. They filled bejeweled silver goblets with a light, sparkling ale with a barm like the froth of a wind-swept sea. It tasted like no ale Robert had drunk before—it was delicious. Robert ate and drank, but he could not enjoy it as the others so obviously did. His mind was racing with questions. He kept flinging them out whenever he could.

"You are an impatient fellow," their host said. "Hardly wolfed down a few bites or quaffed your ale and already you want answers. What happened to the rules of hospitality?"

He let out a huge laugh to show he was not really offended, then stroked his chin, deep in thought.

"This young woman whom you call 'your' lady, happens to be..." He turned and smiled at Una. " ...my granddaughter."

Robert looked at him incredulously, then at Una, who seemed to have been holding her breath the last few minutes. She let it out now with a huge sigh.

"Is this true?"

Una took a deep breath.

"I thought it was just a story. My mother told me many stories when I was a girl. I had long since forgotten them all, but I remember one like this."

"Ah! Your mother!" Their host seemed enraptured, holding a prawn in his fingers. He had been about to put it in his mouth, but now hesitated and instead waved it in the air while he rolled his eyes and tilted back his head in thought, as if tasting a fine wine instead of remembering the past. "Of all my girls, she was perhaps my favorite—if a man is permitted to favor one child over another. She had such a zest, so much—spunk. Naturally, she was headstrong too. It was her undoing, alas!"

He paused, apparently intrigued by something he had just said, as if he hadn't expected to hear himself say it.

"Isn't it strange," he added, "how the things that endear a person to us so often turn out to be their weaknesses. Who, indeed, is ever loved for their virtues? And who, indeed, can truly love perfection?"

"Who are you?" Robert demanded, fairly forcefully this time.

"I am Mananan, of course. Mananan Mac Lir."

The name echoed in Robert's head. Lir, of course, was the ancient Celtic god of the sea. He whom Robert had pronounced dead in the storm. He whose name had been given to the gem. This man, then, claimed to be his son.

Mananan looked at Una, ignoring Robert. He wolfed down the prawn, head, legs, shell and all, and twirled the Stone of Lir in his hand, having removed it from the locket around his neck.

"I gave this precious gem to your mother when she came of age. She wanted to travel—among men. I had no way of knowing when I gave it to her that she would fall in love with a man—your father—and would not merely travel among men, but live with them as well. And no way of knowing either that she would meet so untimely a death and that the stone would fall into the wrong hands and be used for such evil purpose. But there it is—in a nutshell."

He returned the stone to the locket. For a moment there was complete silence, at least between he and Una and Robert— the others were paying little attention (except for Sean— always the curious one) and were preoccupied with their own banter—as well as the food and drink. Seeing Robert and Una had nothing to say Mananan broke the silence between them himself.

"Your mother was"—Mananan fished for the right word, as if he were speaking an unfamiliar language (indeed, he had an unusual accent)— "irresponsible. She didn't keep in touch. She was angry with me because we quarreled over your father. I didn't approve of her marrying him. Perhaps I was wrong, but it was no excuse for what she did. Breaking off contact like that. If she had kept in touch we could have saved her life. Her illness was not so serious if it had been treated properly. The barbaric medicine they used hurt her more than it helped. But we had no way of helping her, and no way either of retrieving the stone or preventing it from getting into the wrong hands."

He drank from his flagon, eyed Una and Robert questioningly. Neither said anything.

"I have been looking for you for a long time," he said, addressing Una. "As soon as I found out your mother had a surviving daughter I did everything I could to track you down. But alas I had nothing to go upon. Until your friend came along. That was a happy accident. One in a million. A pure fluke. Or was it fate? I've never been able to figure out what's the difference between the two."

Mananan turned to Robert and looked him in the eye: "You have a *geis*, my friend, do you not?"

"How do you know that?" Robert finally broke his silence.

"I can see it."

"See it?"

"Yes. It's the Matrix. Always a balance. Fluke or fate? A perfect balance. People think these are different commodities. They're not. It's all the same. All the Matrix. Did she tell you about the Matrix?"

Mananan seemed to be talking more to himself than to anyone else. Robert did not answer.

"Her mother would have told her, but, you see, her mother didn't know. Not really. It's not so easy, not so simple. How did she explain it? As a weaving? A fabric? A warp and a woof? Oh, that's part of it. But oh so simplistic. Like saying a man consists of a mouth and an arse. It misses the point, don't you think? A man's not a worm. Some — maybe. But for most there's more."

Mananan was following his own train of thought, leaping from one concept to the other. Seeing his guest did not follow him, he put down his flagon and tried to explain. A *geis* and an enchantment, he said, had one thing in common, and that was that they were both distortions in the Matrix, both imbalances.

Sometimes, if the *geis* and the enchantment were "compatible," by fluke or fate, or a balance of both, or by corresponding imbalances that balanced each other out, which amounted to the same thing, this would enable a man, or in this case, Robert and his entire retinue, crew and ship, to pass through the enchantment.

Robert understood very little of this, but he was encouraged by Mananan's talkativeness and willingness to answer questions.

"Is it true the stone is cursed?"

"Cursed? Oh no. Not as such. It is merely... contaminated."

Robert stared at him without comprehension.

"Infected... diseased..." Mananan offered.

"A stone? Diseased?"

"No ordinary stone, my friend. It's a traveler's stone. Used for traveling within the Matrix, from level to level, between the worlds."

"What worlds?"

"Of gods and men, of course. Granddaughter, who is this fellow? He seems—daft."

"He is a Christian. They do not believe in gods. They have only one God, and he is his own father, and his mother is a virgin."

There was no mockery in Una's explanation, though it seemed that way to Robert. She was merely reporting factually what she understood.

Mananan stroked his chin, but he resisted the impulse to ask questions. Instead he considered the idea seriously, then nodded his head and stuck out his lower lip as if to say, "It's possible, it's possible."

Once again he examined the stone in the locket.

"We'll have to do something about this. The stone was pure when I gave it to your mother. But it's been messed around with. Quite a clumsy job, really. An amateur. Probably why he left it where it was."

"I still don't understand."

"The stone was used to effect an enchantment. That isn't the natural function of the stone."

"But the spell was broken."

Mananan shook his head. "No. Your *geis* enabled you to pass through the spell. But it did not completely break it. To do that, you would need to purify the stone."

"How does a person do that?"

"There is only one way to purify an infected stone. That is with light." He glanced up at the glass ceiling. "But it is too late for that now. Morning light is best. For now you are my guests. We can take care of business later."

So saying he waved his hand in the air and more servants appeared with more food and more drink. Musicians and acrobats provided entertainment as the light faded and torches were lit. During the course of the evening Mananan seemed to pay special interest in Robert and quizzed him in detail about his expedition, about O'Leary and Edward Bruce and the English king.

Robert, in turn, quizzed Mananan about who he was and got a verbose reply -

"I am Lord of the Western Seas, of all the Seas of Enchantment through which you've sailed, and of all the islands in the sea, and all the worlds under it. I am the keeper, if you will, of all the enchantments of the Western Seas, the guardian of their secrets, the secrets they keep within themselves."

"What secrets?" Robert asked.

"They would not be secrets if I told you."

Mananan folded his arms, a caricature of one whose lips are sealed.

"Why are the seas enchanted, then? Can you tell me that?"

Mananan pulled on his ear.

"Must there be a reason?"

"My Lady Una suffered an enchantment for the spite of a thwarted lover."

"That is not a reason; that is a motive, and an evil one at that."

Mananan took a long pull on his ale and seemed to reflect.

Robert said nothing, sensing Mananan would speak when he was ready. It took several sips of ale before he was.

"The truth is, my friend, the seas are enchanted to keep the likes of you out of them. There are some things it is not meant for men to do, and one of them is to go poking their noses where they don't belong. The Western Seas are not for you."

"But I am here."

"You broke your *geis*. It's nothing to boast of. Though, of course, I owe it to that circumstance that you found my daughter. Just the same, you should have stayed at home; you do not belong here."

Robert gave a huff, growing irritated with Mananan's attitude towards him.

"Nevertheless—you needed me and my *geis*. You could not find your daughter yourself. You could not save her from the spell that kept her prisoner."

"And you—refusing to throw the Stone into the sea. Such a stubborn and possessive man you are! Only when your comrade threw the stone into the sea was all this..." he indicated the hall, and, more expansively the castle and the entire island... "was all this able to manifest itself. If he hadn't have done that you'd all still be lost and I'd never have had my daughter back."

Robert noted that Mananan appeared to know quite a bit more about events than Robert himself had told him. Was he, perhaps, a seer?

"The day will come," Mananan said now in a low voice tinged with sadness, "when all of this will vanish. Already men are trespassing, men like yourself, others, bolder and more aggressive, cutting across the web that holds this fragile world together. For this is a world of the mind, not of coarse matter, and men who come with ignorance, driven by greed and intolerance, will destroy it. The future does not look good, I'm afraid."

With that, Mananan became sullen and silent. Perhaps, Robert thought, he was simply drunk. To Una he said, "Your grandfather's a strange one." But Una said nothing. She herself was lost in thought. Around him the rest of his companions were carousing. He noticed Neill and Brigit sitting together, as they had before on the ship. Brigit was pouring ale into Neill's mouth, and then she leaned over and kissed him. Robert smiled to himself.

Later servants showed everyone to their various quarters. Mananan personally showed Robert and Una to a comfortably furnished room away from the others, then took Una aside. She was gone for some time and Robert, lying down, reflected on the day's events. He thought about the gem and realized, surprised, how badly he wanted it back. He had felt it all evening. Seeing it dangling from Mananan's neck had filled him with rage. But he did not know how to go about getting it back. Mananan was too powerful for him to take it away by force. He could try asserting his claim to it, but he knew that Una had the better claim, and that only by marrying her could he make a claim himself. And only by renouncing Maire as his wife could he marry Una.

Perhaps, in the end, that was what he would do. With this thought in mind, he fell asleep. He was asleep when Una returned. He never had the chance to ask her what she had been discussing with her grandfather.

26

The next morning Robert woke, a beam of sunlight in his eye, and rolled over to find the other side of the bed empty. Vaguely he thought he heard voices. The voices seemed to be coming from over his head, and looking up Robert observed that the room was lit, like the dining hall, by a glass skylight; over his bed was crystal pyramid supported by black pillars. Robert marveled at the construction, the like of which he had never before seen. Then he rose, dressed, and went in search of the origin of the voices he heard.

Outside his room Robert found himself in a corridor. At one end there were stairs which descended to the great hall. At the other end an open door revealed a stairway which led to the roof. Robert ascended and found himself on a spacious, plaza-like area. Skylights, crystal pyramids, dotted the rooftop like mushrooms in a field. A series of pyramids, the roof over the great hall, took up over a third of the area, but between the other less grandiose constructions there were ample pathways, dotted with planters crowded with flowers and shrubs, even trees. The sight was like nothing Robert had ever seen, nor imagined even in the court of the English or French king, or the palaces of popes and emperors. He marveled over the architecture and construction. He could see no cracks in the black stone; the building appeared to be made of one piece.

He wandered down a path, still following the sound of the voices, but absently now, his attention distracted by the spectacle around him. He was almost startled upon turning a corner to find Mananan and Una before him, scanning the ground looking for cracks that continued to elude him.

Mananan was standing in front of a marble table. The table was almost like an altar, and Mananan's attention focused on something on it. Una was seated on a ledge behind him.

"What are you doing?" Robert asked.

"I am purifying the Stone of Lir," Mananan said, without looking up.

Robert glanced at the object in front of Mananan. It shone with an intense light, the effect, Robert concluded, of an array of mirrors standing upon tripods that Mananan had apparently arranged around the table, each directing the light of the sun to the space in front of Mananan, which was itself a sort of concave mirror, like a bowl.

In its center was the Stone, or so Robert assumed; he could see nothing but the intense white light directed upon it so intensely that the gem itself almost seemed to de-materialize, and where it had "been" there was only an intense halo, almost like a hole in the fabric of space.

"Do not gaze directly into the light," Mananan warned.

Only then did Robert, his vision swirling with red spots, notice that Mananan wore a pair of spectacles made of dark glass over his eyes. Robert had never seen anything like them. Together with the long robe he wore, made out of a fine, shiny multicolored material that glistened in the sun, they made him look like some sort of bug-like creature, like a giant bee or wasp.

"To be more correct, I myself am doing nothing. The light does it all. It purifies the Stone. Once it has been cleansed it will work again."

"Work? What exactly, does the Stone do?"

"You think of this as an ordinary gem, something to stick on an emperor's crown or hang between his harlot's tits for decoration. It is no such thing. It is a tool. A very complex apparatus. A key."

"A key? To what?"

"To other worlds. Surely you have noticed, dear friend, that you are not in Ireland. Or any place like it."

"Magic."

"*Ptah*! Magic is just a word for what you don't understand."

Mananan, apparently satisfied the process was complete, began disassembling the mirrors around the table, turning them away so that they no longer caught the rays of the sun. When he had finished he removed his spectacles and picked the gem off the table, holding it in front of him. Its bluish-green light shimmered and grew in strength. As it did so, tentacles of light, like tiny bits of lightning, flickered from it, at first hesitantly, then certainly. The tentacles ran up and down Mananan's arm, some slinking down his robe like silver snakes, disappearing into the floor.

"There is nothing to fear," Mananan said softly. "Here. Take it."

He held the Stone of Lir out to Robert, but Robert, disturbed by the darting fingers of light, drew back. Mananan laughed, as he would at a child. Then, more seriously, he said, "You will need this if you are ever to return home."

Robert glanced at Una. How much had she discussed with Mananan while he slept? And what, exactly, had they discussed? What, for example, did Mananan mean when he said "*you* will need this"? Did he include Una when he spoke of Robert returning "home"? He searched Una's eyes for answers, but she looked away.

"Go ahead. Take it." Mananan repeated.

Robert took the gem hesitantly. As he did so the flickering threads of bluish light that had run over Mananan's body receded, though a few continued to creep up and down Robert's arm, causing him mild consternation.

"What do I do with it?"

"Feel it with your mind. Feel the power of Lir's gem with your mind. Feel it, if you will, running up from your hand, up your arm…"

Even as he spoke Robert saw strands of bluish light run up his arm. Growing in power, the tentacles began to envelop his whole body. As Mananan's voice droned on in a languid monotone, Robert felt his vision fade and the space around him seemed to dissolve into a dark void punctured by points of light that swirled around him like a vortex. These began to trace brilliant lines of yellow, blue and green, and colors Robert had never before seen. The lines formed geometrical shapes that changed before his eyes. He was no longer aware of Una or Mananan. He seemed to be flying; the ground beneath his feet had dissolved at the same time as the walls. The geometrical shapes now formed a sort of roof and floor between which he was propelled by an unknown but unimaginably powerful force at a speed beyond belief. So fast was he propelled that he felt as if his body would be torn apart by the stress, and he pulled himself into a fetal position, keeping his arms and legs tucked close to his body, shielding his head with his hands, closing his eyes and opening them only at intervals, stealing glimpses between his fingers.

Then the geometric shapes too dissolved and he seemed to go into a sort of free fall, though where he was falling he could not say; there was nothing to say what was up or what was down, just a dark void. In the void large spherical shapes appeared. It was hard to guess their size without knowing their distance, but it occurred to Robert, incredible as it seemed, that they were planets, or the heavenly spheres of which the philosophers spoke.

Then something moist and cold brushed past his face, a long wispy cloud. More clouds streaked past him until he found himself looking down upon a landscape of clouds through which at intervals ground could be seen. Suddenly he was overwhelmed with giddiness, feeling intensely vulnerable. He must have fainted, for a brief amnesia wiped every recollection from his mind and he thought for a moment he was lying in his bed in the castle in Kerry, and that he was a boy again and that his mother was singing lullabies in Gaelic. He almost heard her voice, so real it was as if her lips were next to his ear. Then he opened his eyes and saw nothing but a soft mat of whiteness. His feet felt as if they were immersed in a heavy, warm mud. He could barely see his own hand when he held it in front of his eyes; streams of whiteness trickled through his fingers. He found himself thinking of the heavy fog they had encountered before they sighted Una's island. Had he been dreaming? Was everything that had happened all a dream and all the time he had been lost in a fog?

Then another hand took his, fingers materializing out of the air. It was Una's. Not far away Mananan grinned.

"Such is the power of a traveler's stone. A small demonstration, really."

The misty vapors around him began to move in patterns, and the patterns began to congeal before his eyes into solid forms—the floor, the stone 'altar,' the mirrors and their tripods, the skylights on the roof, Una and Mananan. They seemed to materialize from the vapor itself, as if that was all they had ever been. He was back where they had started. Had he ever left? As if reading his mind Mananan said:

"Traveling is not what you suppose. The world's not what you suppose."

Robert felt his feet tremble beneath him.

"I liked the world the way it was."

"We can return you to your world."

Robert looked at him suspiciously. Why was Mananan suddenly so generous?

"And the Lady Una?"

"Una does not belong in your world," Mananan said flatly. His voice was firm, authoritative. But Robert wanted to hear it from Una. He turned and pleaded with his eyes. But she slowly shook her head.

"Sharlaugh was partly right. The years I have spent in enchantment may not effect me here, but in your world, they would. Your world's a different time, not just a different place; it's a bag of bones and dust you'd bring home."

Robert made his decision. He'd already considered the possibility the night before Una threw the stone into the sea. Now he was sure.

"Then I shall stay here."

Something flickered in Una's eyes. Then she seemed to

hesitate— "No, you mustn't. I can't let you," her eyes said now. But she did not have the chance to speak. Mananan spoke first.

"That's impossible! Absurd!" Mananan sputtered. There was surprise, as well as anger in his voice. With a visible effort he attempted a more reasoned approach.

"Don't you see? There would be nothing for you here."

"There would be my Lady Una, your granddaughter. Without Una I do not wish to return. Besides, it is my own world which holds nothing for me. I see that now. A life of conflict and hypocrisy. Empty loyalties, loveless marriages. I had to come here to see that, but I am certain now. Return the others, but leave me here. Surely in this vast sea, with all your islands, there is room for me."

Mananan seemed genuinely moved, but he also furrowed his brow, troubled.

"You say that without truly knowing. Your feelings are noble and do you credit, but they will not stand the test."

"I say they will," Robert replied, at the same time wondering what test Mananan could have in mind.

"We shall see," Mananan said.

Robert was about to challenge Mananan as to what he meant by that when Una, observing something above them, shouted— "Look!"

Above them a huge bird circled, descending. As it descended Robert recognized it. So did Una.

"Umalekie!" she cried, and waved.

Umalekie landed with a swirl of dust which was raised up by his powerful wings.

"Whycome you leave us like that?" he whined. "We was worried about you."

"And I about you," Una said, stroking his feathered head affectionately. "But I figured you'd find us soon enough."

Umalekie gave an account of how, after being hit in the head by MacFael's well-aimed stone, he had watched the island emerge from the sea from his perch on the yardarm. At first he wondered if he were suffering from concussion and seeing things. He'd closed his eyes, trying to get a grip. He must have blacked out, for when he had opened his eyes again he found the ship deserted. After spending the night alone recuperating he flew off in the morning, and seeing the castle not far away he decided to come and have a look, though he wasn't sure what he'd have done if he hadn't spotted them on the roof; the castle looked much too foreboding to just go up and knock on the front door.

"We thoughts you was dead," he added.

"As I fully expected to be," Una said, and began to explain everything to Umalekie as if he were an old friend she had not seen for years.

Mananan, meanwhile, clapped his hands together, declaring himself to be ravenously hungry.

"Shall we all assemble in the great hall for eggs and ham? And then... well, you are my guests, and I your host. These other matters we can work out as between friends.

27

While they were waiting for breakfast Robert discussed his plans with the others. "You're mad!" bellowed Reginald.

MacErin was more emphatic, accusing Robert of desertion. "A fine day it is when leaders desert their men. I thought it was usually the other way around."

Only Neill seemed ambivalent, saying, "If you stay, I stay." Robert looked at him bemusedly. He wondered if his willingness to stay had to do with Brigit. But it was one thing for Robert himself to stay for the love of a woman. It was another thing for Neill. He was still young, and Robert had an obligation to make sure he returned home.

"No, I cannot allow that," he said. "You must return with the others." After which Neill became sullen and contrary.

Earlier, with Una beside him, Robert had been exuberant and enthused with his own certainty. But his comrades whittled away at this bit by bit. The more he defended his plans the less certain he became, the more hollow it all sounded. Una said nothing, and her silence ate away at his certainty even more. Why was she not more supportive? Somehow when he tried to visualize staying behind with Una in these strange seas, the others returning to Ireland, he could not see it. He thought of Maire (to whom he had made eternal vows), his unborn son (whom he would never see), of O'Leary (who would curse him for deserting) of his poor old mother (who would mourn him as if he were dead), and he could not see how he could go through with it. Equally, however, he could not visualize leaving Una behind (as if, indeed, this had all been a dream from which one wakes).

His own uncertainty and indecisiveness perplexed him and he became suddenly silent and broody. He had always been a decisive man, even bold and daring by reputation. Now he felt helpless to find a way out of this relatively simple conundrum — stay or go?

After breakfast Mananan announced that baths had been prepared for the guests, and that barbers would be provided for those who wanted them. Una herself trimmed Robert's hair, leaving a "culan," or small lock of hair at the back, but cutting the rest short, and Brigit brought perfumed oil. Everyone was provided fresh, clean clothes, and in due time they all reconvened in the dining hall to continue the feast.

Mananan, himself refreshed and clothed in his multicolored garments, presided, jovial as ever, radiant with the elan expected of a good host. He pointed to each delicacy on the table, describing both it and the culinary techniques used to prepare it. He waved to the servants to pour wine and ale for all, and sat down to partake of the feast himself, lest any holding back from politeness awaiting his own participation.

Robert asked Mananan to explain in greater detail what were the powers of the gem. Where had he been when he imagined himself flying? What really had happened? Had he really traveled, or only imagined it?

"You really traveled," Mananan said. "To us here, Una and I, you became just a blur for a moment. Then you returned. You were only gone a moment, the blink of an eye, but you were gone."

Mananan removed the jewel from the locket around his neck and held it up for all to see.

"You can go anywhere. Anywhere in the universe. You are limited only by your imagination. Where would you like to go?"

Robert sensed once again that Mananan was trying to get rid of him.

"I told you," he replied, again defiant. "I wish to go nowhere. I wish to stay here."

Among Robert's companions, however, there was a chorus of "Ireland!" Donegal!" and "Ulster!" Umalekie, who was also present as Mananan's guest, spoke his own wish with his eyes— "Home." Mananan laughed. He now seemed to be in a quite jovial mood.

"As you wish. To *each* as they wish. But first, a small demonstration."

Mananan ordered the table in front of him cleared, then placed the Stone of Lir in the center of the cleared area. As everyone gathered around to look the Stone began to radiate, then emitted a cloud of vapor which covered the surface of the table to a diameter of several feet. This then became opaque and glass-like. Marbled patterns swirled just beneath the surface, almost as if it were alive.

"Behold."

As they watched the opaque surface shimmered and became transparent. They found themselves staring down as if from a height of thousands of feet on a land green and wide. A sudden feeling of vertigo possessed Robert, standing as he was closest to the table.

"Don't worry," Mananan said, seeing his predicament. "It's just an image."

"An image of what?"

"Ireland, of course. The land you have forsaken forever."

Suddenly Una, sensing a devious stratagem on Mananan's part, stood and shouted: "No!"

Mananan seemed almost amused, seemingly indifferent to his granddaughter's anguish.

"If your friend truly has made the decision to stay, there can be no harm in showing him what he is leaving. Unless..."

"Unless what?" Robert asked.

"You are afraid."

"I am not afraid. You said yourself it is only an image."

Mananan seemed amused by this: "Only an image?"

Looking down and overcoming his vertigo Robert saw three columns of men marching in a rough formation, each separated by several miles so that no one column was in ready touch with the other. They formed the vanguard, mainguard and rearguard of an army. In front of them another army was massed to meet them. Quickly Robert surmised the situation.

"They are walking into a trap! The vanguard will be surrounded and annihilated before the mainguard can come to their assistance. They've allowed too much distance between the wings. After the vanguard is annihilated the mainguard is next. And then the rearguard."

Mananan looked and nodded indifferently. Apparently he saw the same scene Robert saw.

"I daresay you are right."

Robert strained his eyes to make out the banners. To his surprise the more he strained his eyes the closer it all seemed. He was able to identify the opposing army as English, and the three columns as Scots and Irish. He was even able to recognize some faces in the army of Irish, and there, in the vanguard was none other than O'Leary himself, leading a troop of Irish in which, Robert realized with chagrin, he himself ought to be included. MacErin saw him too, and grabbed MacFael. Both tensed with anticipation.

"I must be there. With the vanguard."

"There? But you said..." It was play-acting on Mananan's part, pretending to be surprised by Robert's sudden change of heart when all the while he had staged this little demonstration precisely to entrap him.

He dispensed with the play-acting now: "Did I not tell you you are limited only by your imagination?"

It was a question of loyalties, though. Loyalties, alliances, vendettas and blood feuds — ties that bound. Hate was stronger than love. Malice stronger than self-interest. Robert was hardly aware of Una's presence as he chronicled the obsession that, she realized now, would inevitably part them.

It is the way with men. Mananan shrugged, a limp apology to Una. Offer a man the universe. Such things are wasted. Squandered. Look at MacFinn. You thought this man was different. But men are the same. It is why we live apart.

"That is O'Leary," Robert continued, trying to justify why he had to get to Ireland this very minute when only moments ago he swore he had forsaken his homeland forever. "I made a promise. I promised a *kern* of good fighting men."

"Your companions, you mean?"

Mananan looked at the retinue assembled now around the table.

"Aye. We were to meet O'Leary in Donegal, thence to Ulster to join the Scots."

"Well, a good thing for you you didn't make that rendezvous."

"Why good?"

"You just said yourself they would be cut to pieces."

"If I can warn them they might have a chance. They must pull back and let the mainguard catch up with them. Then, if they can hold off the English, and if the rearguard were to do a flanking move, they can strike the English where they are weakest—snatch victory from defeat."

Mananan regarded the various positions, stroking his beard and thrusting out his lower lip. "I think you misjudge the timing. The English are upon them."

"You don't know the Irish. They fight best when they are desperate, and their lack of armor gives them great mobility. If they mounted a series of hit-and-run raids, mounted Irish with spears and slings, they could delay the English."

"I do know the Irish. But they are not just desperate, they are also disparate." Mananan laughed at his own pun, seemingly unmoved by the plight of the men below. "A far more serious matter, in my opinion. And the English have them outnumbered two to one. But, of course, I am not a military man."

"Indeed you are not. The numbers mean nothing. That's the magic battles turn upon."

"Ah! Now it's magic you speak of!"

Mananan's sarcasm was undisguised, but Robert didn't notice; he was in a frenzy. Already he could feel the fierce blood of battle rising. So clearly could he visualize what needed to be done that he could not bear the thought of being a mere spectator.

"All they need is half a chance. I could give them that. Just half a chance. Can you get me down there? Now?"

"Down there? Me?"

Robert wondered if Mananan were playing a game with him. But it was becoming clearer to him now. He remembered the feeling he had always had when holding the Stone of Lir, the feeling of power, the feeling that all things were possible, the feeling of *decisiveness*. And there was his experience on the castle roof when, holding the Stone, he had thought he had traveled the breadth of the universe. Traveling to Ireland, by comparison, was a small matter.

Now the mystical artifact lay on the table directly in front of him. Mananan had seen him gazing upon it with consuming fascination and the look of understanding in Mananan's eyes gave Robert a sudden certainty and resolve.

"Go ahead. Do it!" Mananan's eyes seemed to say.

Robert made a broad sweep with his hand and scooped it off the table.

As he did so Una, who had understood in the same instant what he was doing, cried out, "No!" and tried to intercept him. Even as his hands closed around the Stone, Una's hand, smaller and less strong, but no less determined, closed over his own.

28

Robert felt himself tumbling head-over-heels as if through a dimly lit tunnel. As he emerged from the darkness branches lashed his face. He hit soft ground with a force that knocked the wind out of him. Gasping for air he sat up. Immediately he was aware that he was no longer in possession of the Stone. Thinking that he must have dropped it he made a quick, desperate search in the leaves at his feet, at the same time becoming aware that he had landed directly in front of the advancing vanguard and that several Irish had already surrounded him, threatening him with their spears. O'Leary, galloped over, riding bareback, and recognizing his old friend, reined up, simultaneously sliding off his horse with an agility only the Irish had.

"Robert!" he bellowed. "Why never have I seen such an entrance. Upon my word, I'd swear you fell out of the sky. Were you...?"

O'Leary surveyed the tall dogwood bush through which Robert had come crashing to the ground, trying to figure out how Robert had done what he seemed to have done.

"Are you mad?" Robert blurted, still poking the ground, looking for the Stone.

"Say what?"

"You've overreached the mainguard."

"And have I indeed?" O'Leary continued staring up at the spindly tip of the dogwood, still waving from side to side, trying to figure where Robert had fallen from. "I suppose you're going to be telling me you surveyed my position from up... there."

He pointed to the bush, many branches of which were now bent or broken.

"You might say I have, though I've no time to explain. And from what I have seen I can tell you that you've got about as much brains as a cow."

"Oh! Is it insults already?"

"Where's the mainguard?"

"Behind me, of course. Or have you such a great view from your bush that you know something I don't know?"

"You haven't a clue where your mainguard is because you haven't bothered to keep in touch, and you don't know the English are waiting just around the corner because you haven't bothered to send scouts."

"Are they really, now? Well then—this is it, isn't it? Better..."

O'Leary glanced at Robert's side.

"My friend, you've come without your sword, and you're dressed like you've come direct from a wedding. Do I smell perfume?"

Robert, who had not really ceased poking the ground with his foot to find the Stone now patted his side, suddenly remembering he had removed his sword in the dining hall. O'Leary was shouting orders to his men, preparing them for battle.

"And where is your horse? And the fighting men you promised me? My God, man, and you lecture me about scouts? Ha!"

"No sword. No horse. No men. I bring only myself."

"No horse? What, did you fly?" O'Leary laughed a great guffaw.

"No time to explain," Robert grunted, giving up his search. "Look, you must fall back. Immediately."

"Fall back? Why my ears must deceive me, upon my word. Is this the Robert I thought I knew?"

O'Leary grabbed a spare sword from his horse, and tossed it to Robert. Then he shouted for someone to bring a horse as well.

"For God's sake, man. You must buy some time. You must reconnoiter with the mainguard and the rearguard."

O'Leary spat. "Let them reconnoiter with us. If they want a share in the glory."

"Glory? Don't you see you'll be cut to pieces?"

O'Leary ignored this. The famous O'Leary bravado was mind boggling. Robert had witnessed it in action before. It had always worked. But this time Robert was not so sure.

"Where are your men? You promised me a *kern*."

"And so I had them, too. Six, at least. And would have got more, but they... got left behind, I'm afraid. I've no time to explain, and doubt you'd believe a word of it..."

"Neill...?"

"He was with me. Just not here...but he's safe."

It was all O'Leary wanted to hear. He became suddenly serious, and took Robert by the forearm in an embrace.

"Man, you can tell me everything when it's all over. Get me drunk. For now I'm just glad you're here. It'll be like old times. Fighting back-to-back."

He didn't have a chance to say any more. There was a loud commotion just ahead, and a wave of shouting and screaming from all directions. The vanguard had engaged the English. The die was cast and there was nothing to do but watch it rattle and roll and play with the fate of men. O'Leary, quickly mounting his horse, dashed off towards the action, beckoning Robert to follow.

A squire had led a horse up to Robert. Even as Robert mounted it, it was shot from under him. The English had their archers. And knights, as well, if the thunderous pounding of hooves was any indication. As Robert was struggling to his feet a knight thundered past him, sword flashing. Robert just barely had a chance to raise his own sword to ward off the blow. In doing so he caught his heel on the neck of his dying horse and fell over backwards. The English knight ignored him, perhaps thinking him disposed of, and charged on.

An arrow whizzed by Robert's head. The quill buzzed like a wasp, licking the lobe of his ear. Another knight was barreling towards him, lance lowered. Robert tried to assess the situation quickly. How many were there? Where were they coming from? Where were the archers firing from? But there was no time. There was only time to dodge the lance and avoid the thundering hooves.

This time the English knight reined in. He turned his horse around, threw down the awkward lance and drew his sword. He had recognized in Robert someone worth killing. An Anglo-Norman. Not just an Irish or a Scot. A traitor.

But then something strange and unexpected happened. In front of the knight, and a bit to his left, there was a peculiar distortion; the air itself seemed to flutter like a banner in the breeze, and suddenly there stood none other than Reginald. Reginald's broadsword flashed and with one stroke decapitated the knight's horse. The next stroke cleaved the knight himself from the neck to the navel.

Even while this was happening MacFael and MacErin appeared in the same manner, followed by Sean and last of all Neill, who looked a little dazed. It was Neill's first taste of real combat.

To be thrown into the midst of such a bedlam... it wasn't fair.

Reginald, extracting his sword from the slain English knight, turned to Robert and bellowed.

"What do you mean leaving us like that?"

He'd barely finished his sentence when an arrow caught him in the throat. Robert, reacting swiftly, retraced the arrow's path and located its source—a group of bowmen in the woods were wreaking havoc on the Irish with impunity.

"There!" he shouted to MacErin and MacFael, even as Reginald staggered and crumpled to his knees. But the archers in the woods were quicker than thought itself. No sooner did MacErin and MacFael, on Robert's cue, locate the danger than a swarm of arrows cut them down too.

Meanwhile Neill, who should have had the chance, at least once in his short life, to acquit himself in battle face-to-face with his enemy, instead stood among his fallen comrades, confused, facing now this way, now that, holding his sword in front of him as if fighting a phantom. Robert could only watch helplessly as he too took an arrow, then another, and reeled helplessly. He would have been better off, Robert reflected bitterly, in so far as there was time for reflection at such a time, having stayed with Brigit as he had no doubt really desired all along.

Sean had disappeared. Perhaps he had found a hole in which to hide. Perhaps he too had been cut down.

Robert felt a strange, salty taste in his mouth. It was blood. At the same time he noticed the ground doing strange things. Staggering, he pulled at an arrow in his chest, snapping it off. Stupid, he thought. It would be more difficult now to extract. But then, what difference did it make? He knew a mortal wound when he saw it. He'd taken it in his lung. He would suffocate in his own blood. Falling to his knees he tried to collect his thoughts.

Thoughts. How do you collect thoughts? he asked himself. Beneath him a man lay in the grass dying. The man was himself. Could he collect himself? He wanted to laugh, but he felt such an emptiness. To laugh one needed breath, and life.

Then something incongruous happened. A large bird—no, it was not a bird, it was a man with very large, powerful wings—descended from the sky and landed beside the body of the man who was himself. Robert felt huge talons gently lift him. In a moment he was being transported into the sky. He could hear the beating of mighty wings over his head. At the same time he heard voices murmuring around him. He closed his eyes and surrendered himself to the sensation of floating.

29

"May I assume it was not the Archangel Gabriel, but the manbird who plucked you from the field? Otherwise you would not be here, but..."

The Abbot makes a gesture with his finger indicating heaven. His voice is weary. The light that had fringed the heavy curtain is gone. Outside it will be dusk.

"You are correct. He returned me to Mananan's castle where Lady Una used her medicines to treat my wounds. Without this I would surely have died; the wound should have been fatal."

His recollection of this is hazy. He imagines it as if he was looking through fine gauze, the kind they make in Palestine that you can see through but which makes everything blurry and indistinct.

The way things actually looked when he opened his eyes after the battle, after Umalekie had brought him back to Mananan's castle. He had barely been able to make out Una's face. But her voice—that was crystal clear, more precious and beautiful that the stone itself, like a gem. She was singing the song he'd first heard her sing the first night at the banquet:

> Still do I linger by
>   The shore, and venture
> The portents of the sea
>   Will give some sign of thee.
>
> I'll wait there 'til it does
>   I'll look in sea and sky
> In wind, in waves, in stars,
> Until you come to me.

Whatever time had passed, whether in reality or in enchantment, whether in dream or in life, seemed to hang in the air around him, dissipating. A cool breeze blew through the window, ruffling the curtains, and outside the window birds were singing.

Seeing that he was awake Una leaned over him, placing her hand on his forehead to check for fever, and looking deeply and lovingly into his eyes.

Her gaze was like a sweet wine to him, refreshing him and raising his spirits. Then images, ugly and horrible, flashed through his mind. He was remembering. He made a sudden move to sit up, and pain stabbed him in the chest. Una restrained him from further exertions with a firm but gentle hand.

"Neill? Is Neill...?" He knew the answer. He had seen what he had seen. But seeing was not enough. He needed to be told.

"Dead. I'm sorry."

"MacErin? Reginald... the others?"

"Dead, all dead."

Robert sank back into the pillow.

"I'm so sorry," she repeated.

He sighed: "It was what they enlisted for. The hazards of war. It's how they would have wanted it."

His response seemed callous. Una could not accept it.

"I can't believe you care nothing for them."

"I did not say that. I meant that a noble death is better than..." He left his sentence unfinished. Una finished it for him in her mind.

"Than what? Than this?" She cast a quick glance around them, suggesting not just the room in which they were, but the whole world of enchantment in which the room and the black castle of Mananan, and the sea itself, all existed.

"Better than to watch the spectacle like a sightseer. Better than to say: 'I was lost in an enchantment, and couldn't find my way out of it. I saw the battle through a looking glass. Too bad how it turned out.'"

Una bit her lip.

"Better than that."

The strain of speaking hurt his chest. Even the vibrations of his voice, which seemed coarser than he remembered, were like a hot rake inside his lungs. At the same time a dark hand reached over his consciousness. He surrendered himself to it, finding rest and oblivion. Slipping casually from one level of consciousness to another, in and out of wakefulness, he picked up bits and pieces of what had happened from things that Una told him. He would emerge from sleep for brief periods and she would talk to him in a quiet voice while doing embroidery.

She was responsible for sending the others. She had managed to wrest the stone out of his hand even as he had passed back into his own world and met up with O'Leary. He would have dragged her with him, with fatal results, had not Mananan pulled her back himself. Distraught, she had insisted that Mananan send the others after Robert. "You must save him!" she had cried. She would have gone herself, but Mananan would not let her.

Finally, when everything had failed, when Reginald, MacErin, Neill and MacFael, all lay dead, and Robert himself was mortally wounded, all of which Una watched, Umalekie volunteered to bring Robert back.

30

Over the next few days, which seemed like years, Robert gradually emerged from the dark forgetfulness in which his mind had sunk. He gained strength in body, sat up in bed, took sustenance and, sooner than he could have hoped, was able to walk. It was nothing less than a miracle for a man so close to death as he had been, and he attributed it all to Una's medicine, and her constant care. Never had she left his side.

When he was well enough they walked along the upper perimeters of the black castle, gazing out over the island. From here they could survey all points of view. Though still weak Robert experienced everything more intensely than he had before, and despite being in mourning because of Neill he could not repress a bubbling sense of elation and joy, as if he'd been reborn. Only days before he had been in a dark forgetfulness, yet today his eyes saw the world in more vibrant colors than he had ever imagined: The sea a brilliant turquoise, the sky a deep azure, the sand of the beach a gleaming gold, the trees and grass a lush green. So it was surprising that, with such heightened perception, he at first did not notice that the *Black Sligo* was gone.

"Grandfather sent it back. The crew. Together with the pilot. But he kept the treasure, and neither Tom nor the crew will remember anything. As far as they will be concerned they took you and your retinue to Donegal."

"Mananan put a spell on their memories. Is that what you are saying?"

"Yes, you could put it that way."

"I could, could I?" Like Mananan she treated words as if

they were no more than convenient markers. We agree to let a word stand for this, stand for that. If it pleases us to do so. Had she always spoken that way, or was it something she had learned to do since being here with her grandfather?

The ground where the ship had been still bore the mark of the keel. Yet there was no sign of it having been dragged to the shore. Robert and Una walked down to survey the spot, but he saw no sense in asking questions. More magic? If we chose to call it that.

"Then there is no going back." Robert said this as if it were something he were resigned to, but in fact he was glad. Glad too that the decision had been made for him and did not require him to weigh the alternatives as he had had to do before.

"No. He will send you back as well."

Her use of the word "will" took him by surprise.

"I don't want to go back."

"You must."

"And you?"

"I have told you—it is impossible for me. Time has stolen my world. What Sharlaugh said... what I feared when MacErin threw the Stone into the sea... was true."

She made a motion with her fingers of something crumbling into dust.

"Yes," he said, remembering the story of Oisin. Perhaps that was Oisin's mistake. He returned. But he did not have to.

"No. You must," she repeated. She was emphatic. "There is still time for you if you return now. Later it will be too late. Take the gem. It is of no use to me here anyway. With it you can return to your time. And it will fetch a great price. You will be a wealthy and powerful man."

He shook his head. "I too have lost everything. Neill. O'Leary. All my companions. All dead. I too should have died on the field of battle. So let it be. Let me be considered dead. Dead to that world, but alive to this."

"You have a wife. And a son."

"A son?"

"Your wife named him Rory."

"Her father's name. We had agreed our first born male would have her father's name. But how do you know this?"

"While you were recovering—" She smiled coyly. He understood. Just as the Stone had enabled Robert to see the battle, so Una had used the Stone to spy on his wife, Maire. She could see things, but not actually travel there.

"She's nice—your wife. She loves you."

"How do you know that?"

She shrugged. "You were in her thoughts."

"You cannot read a person's thoughts."

"She spoke of you."

"It is not the same—words and thought. Especially words and love. A wife is expected to speak of her husband at such times. She is a good wife. But I don't think love is involved. It is you I love."

"And your son? Is there no father's love for him?"

Una's mood suddenly changed and her eyes flashed with anger.

"Love. Don't speak of words and love to me. You do not love me. You don't know what love is. You are a heartless man."

The words stung him. He did not know what to say, and she was not finished.

"I tell you, I do not understand you. You say you wish to stay with me, that you love me. Yet, you left so you could fight a futile battle. You were prepared to throw your life away. You did not think of me then. Now, you want to throw it away again, and you do not think of your wife and son. You are heartless. I love you, I don't know why, but you are heartless, and cruel..."

Her voice cracked and she hid her face. He reached to touch her hand, but she withdrew it.

"A man has loyalties."

His voice was weak. The words rattled inside his empty chest. *Heartless. Cruel....*

"Love has loyalties. It's hate and malice you speak of, not loyalties. English kings and Scots' kings and Irish kings..."

He felt confused. Nothing seemed to be coming out the way he intended.

"I didn't mean to hurt you."

"But you lied to me. And I cannot trust you now. Never."

"The night we met, the night of the banquet, the night we first made love, I was... confused. I remembered nothing of my life. I—"

"Yes, that was the enchantment. It does that. But you said you would take me back to Ireland—to be your wife. What did you propose to do with me—really?"

"I don't know. It didn't matter. I would have thought of something."

"It did matter. You should have told me."

Robert could not argue with her. "You are right. Forgive me."

"I forgive you."

For a moment his hope soared. But she had not finished.

"But I cannot forget. Nor can I ever be certain if you are here, or whether in your heart you are there and will not again forsake me as you did before. And really, Grandfather is right—you do not belong here. It would be a lie to pretend you do, and a man who lives a lie deceives himself as well as those he loves."

31

A novice brings in a candle. The warm glow makes the Abbot's face seem softer than it is.

"Shall I bring supper, Father?"

"I shall take supper later. We are almost finished. You will stay the night, I presume? Yes? See that a room is prepared for our guests, and see that there is a place at the table for him and his son."

Waving the novice away the Abbot turns back to Sir Robert. "Perhaps you will join me for midnight mass?"

Robert nods, though he is tired and is thinking more of sleep than of masses.

"You still have the Stone of Lir?"

The Abbot's question takes Robert by surprise.

"Yes, I have it with me now." *Robert fumbles with the purse at his waist, and takes out the stone, holding it up for the Abbot to see. The Abbot, on Robert's encouragement, takes the gem in his hand.*

The Abbot sucks in his breath. If he had thought that Robert had exaggerated in the telling of the tale, such doubts are instantly dispelled by the material piece of reality that Robert produces from his purse. Even in the dim light of the Abbot's office the stone shines with an almost surreal light. It's size, and its unusual color and brilliance, makes it without a doubt the most beautiful object the Abbot has ever seen. Not that the Abbot cares much for beautiful objects. No material, worldly object can compare in value to the simple purity of a man's uncorrupted soul, be that man a peasant or a king. But even the Abbot, face-to-face with such a gem, cannot help but forget momentarily the more spiritual training and obligations of his office.

"How does it—work?"

"It doesn't. It may be I simply don't know how. It may be

Mananan played some trick on me. To keep me from going back, as he must have known I would if I could. He distrusted me and would have done anything to keep me from going back."

"Would you have?" The Abbot caresses the stone and continues to examine it. As beautiful and priceless as it may be, could it be magical as well? The Abbot's naturally skeptical mind begins to work.

"If a wish could be real, I'd have done so long ago. My life has been nothing but a hollow shell and a lie since then."

"You call your life a lie? It seems a harsh judgment."

The Abbot has made harsher judgments himself.

"But deserved, alas. It is my own folly has made it so. I blame no one but myself."

His marriage to Maire had indeed been a loveless one, whatever Una may have thought she sensed. When he had returned home after his adventure, even the priceless stone he carried secretly in his pouch seemed a dead and useless thing, like his own heart.

"You've changed," Maire said. "It's not just Neill. Not just O'Leary and the battle. It's something else."

But he refused to talk about it. She would only think him mad if he told her. Feeling rejected, Maire withdrew herself. As if to make a statement about the sterility of their relationship she never conceived again. Their son, Rory, was their only offspring.

"But the gem could have made you wealthy beyond your wildest dreams. With such wealth you could have become powerful, perhaps..." the Abbot makes an expansive gesture with his hands, indicating he is deliberately exaggerating, "... even made yourself king of all Ireland. God knows Ireland needs a king, someone to unite it. The man who possessed such a jewel—" Again, the Abbot makes a sweeping gesture, but is interrupted by Robert.

"Ah, but there's the rub isn't it?"

"Explain."

"The man who used the Stone as you suggest would no longer possess it. That man could only acquire wealth and power by selling the gem. And then he would no longer possess it."

The Abbot nods, intrigued by the irony of possessing something that was of use only if one gave up its ownership. MacFinn had faced the same problem, and taken the opposite course. Yet, he wonders, if the

Stone of Lir were no longer of any use in itself, having no power, why keep it?

Robert tries to explain: "Perhaps it was merely sentimental. Perhaps, on the other hand—?"

The Abbot begins to grow suspicious. "Why, really, did you come here? Did you think perhaps I have some chart that will show you the way to this island? To help you find your way back into the enchantment? What makes you think I would assist you in such a search? I am sworn to seek God, not help others chase illusions!"

Robert says nothing. His silence incriminates him. He had, in fact, made a point of tracking down the pilot. It was the first thing he did after having made the pilgrimage to the shrine of the Virgin. He had a notion of putting to sea and sailing west. If they had sailed there once, could they not sail there again? But Tom remembered nothing. Just as Una said he would, he suffered complete amnesia. In fact, he was entirely convinced that he had taken Robert and his entire retinue to Donegal, whence they had proceeded to their fate in Ulster. When Robert tried to refresh his memory Tom looked at him as if he were mad. In time Robert wondered if indeed he were not. Perhaps that was why he had come to see the Abbot. He needed someone to tell him he was not mad.

The Abbot sighs, and rubs his eyes, placing the gem in front of him on the desk.

"My son. I have many charts. They show many things, probably none of them real—including the Land Promised to the Saints, including isles of fire and isles of ice, and islands of birds and undersea islands and enchantments upon enchantment upon enchantment. Like mirrors set against each other, showing images upon images, forever. Illusion. Nothing but illusion."

Robert stares at him. He can't believe the Abbot would be so dismissive after having listened so long and so attentively.

"But Father, this was real. As real as..." he nods towards the luminescent treasure lying on the desk in front of the Abbot. "As real as that."

Again the Abbot picks up the gem, examining it. Then he closes his eyes and holds it to his breast. He remains like this for several moments, then lets out another sigh, this one deep and profound, dropping the hand in which he holds the Stone of Lir to his lap. He does not open his eyes but seems to be in some state of deep meditation and rest.

"Father?" Robert says, after a long pause. The Abbot opens his eyes, but still says nothing for several moments. Then he passes the precious keepsake across the desk. It is a heavy, reluctant gesture, unlike the dismissive manner that has characterized much of the Abbot's attitude before now.

Robert picks up the Stone and returns it to his purse. He waits, expecting the Abbot to say something.

"You are wrong to concern yourself overmuch with reality, my son. Enchantments, by their nature, deceive us with the appearance of reality."

"Father, can you be sure?"

"My son, I can be sure of nothing, except only that through Jesus Christ are we saved."

He stands up from behind his desk and stretches.

"I have spent my life listening to such tales as yours, and I tell you this: The sea is an empty circle of yearning. A wise man looks within his soul, not towards the world's changing horizons. Forget this enchanted island, forget the enchanted seas, forget this maiden you believe you loved, forget this land of miracles and wonder. Mananan, whether he is a god or a dream, was right—men have no business there. Forget it all. If you do not you will find one day you have left part of your soul there on that enchanted island, and a man with only part of his soul, that man will never find rest or salvation."

"But Father, I need to be sure. I need to know."

"No, my son. You do not need to know. You need to believe. Only to believe. If you believe, and believe in your heart, God will answer you truly. That is really all I can say."

The Abbot walks to the door and opens it.

"Now, good bye. It is late and I have other things to do. I found your story most... interesting, and I am glad you came. But there is nothing more I can do or say."

"Wait! What do you mean 'God will answer?'"

"If I knew that I would not be an Abbot, but a saint and a prophet. Leave it to God how he answers."

32

A novice leads Sir Robert to a cell where two cots have been prepared for Sir Robert and his son. Rory is waiting, sitting on his bed and cutting notches in the wooden frame with his knife.

"A bell will sound for supper," the novice says. "If there's anything else you need, I can be found down the hall."

Robert, exhausted from his meeting with the Abbot, throws himself onto his cot and, folding his arms behind his head, shuts his eyes. For some time there is silence between father and son. Then Robert becomes aware of an expectation that hangs in the stillness. He opens his eyes and finds Rory regarding him intently.

Robert has never told Rory the purpose of his visit to the Abbey, and Rory, being a quiet, respectful boy who has been brought up to mind his own business, has never asked. Now, however, he looks his father in the eye and asks: "Why did you come here to see the Abbot? Does it have something to do with what happened the year I was born?"

His directness takes Sir Robert by surprise and he wonders if the boy knows more than he should.

"What do you mean?"

"I mean Uncle O'Leary. Mother always said..."

Rory looks at the floor. The fact that the young lad is speaking about such things at all is unusual. He has to fight all his natural inclinations to ask such direct questions of his father.

"Your mother always said what?"

"That you were never the same after Uncle O'Leary was killed."

"Did she?"

"She did." The boy swallows. It was the most direct and assertive thing he has ever said to his father.

Sir Robert wonders exactly what Maire told him. That his father *had stopped loving her? The marriage had never been a love match to begin with, though Robert always sensed that Maire had quickly developed for him a love which he had never reciprocated. Or had she told Rory that he had returned from the war muttering crazy things in his sleep, telling tall tales when he'd had too much to drink, accosting fishermen and interrogating them about what they might have seen in a fog, or what tales other fishermen had to tell about what they had seen, and whether it was real or whether it was illusion?*

"You are right. I did come here to talk to the Abbot about that."

He says no more. Rory nods as his father again closes his eyes. He knows that when his father is ready to say more, he will. Meanwhile, he lies down himself, almost as if he is imitating his father. Hands folded behind his head, eyes closed, keeping inside himself his own secrets. Like his father.

33

One more thing the Abbot says before Robert leaves. After the midnight mass he personally walks Robert to his cell.

"I have heard a lot of stories, about a lot of different places, and I've heard a lot of speculation, and indulged in some myself. Some say the whole of the Western Seas is enchanted, and some also that one day the enchantment will all be broken. Then it will be as if the fog lifted for all of us, just as it lifted for you, and all these islands and even the Land Promised to the Saints will be there for us to sail to just as today we sail to England or France.

"But I don't know if this would be a good idea. I'm not sure these places would be the same afterwards. Without the spell of magic, they'd just be bits of land. I wonder if our own world would be the same. Or would it be a little less, a little poorer? I wonder if the world does not need the lure of enchantment. Perhaps our fondness for legends and ancient lore, stories of myth and magic, has to do with our need for assurance that the spiritual realm does exist, that there is more to the world—and ourselves—than meets the eye."

So saying, he goes to his own quarters, and Sir Robert goes to his.

Rory, he knows, will be awaiting his return. He has much to tell his son.

The End

ABOUT THE AUTHOR

James R. Field studied history at the University of British Columbia and religion at McMaster University. As a writer he has used Irish, Greek, and Native North American Mythology to explore the role of alternate realities in our relation to the world. Seas of Enchantment is his first full length novel and blends historical fiction with fantasy.

ABOUT GREATUNPUBLISHED.COM

www.greatunpublished.com is a website that exists to serve writers and readers, and to remove some of the commercial barriers between them. When you purchase a GreatUNpublished title, whether you order it in electronic form or in a paperback volume, the author is receiving a majority of the post-production revenue.

A GreatUNpublished book is never out of stock, and always available, because each book is printed on-demand, as it is ordered.

A portion of the site's share of profits is channeled into literacy programs.

So by purchasing this title from GreatUNpublished, you are helping to revolutionize the publishing industry for the benefit of writers and readers.

And for this we thank you.